# MR BAZALGETTE'S AGENT

# MR BAZALGETTE'S AGENT

LEONARD MERRICK

———

With an Introduction by Mike Ashley

THE BRITISH LIBRARY

This edition published in 2013 by

The British Library
96 Euston Road
London NW1 2DB

Originally published in London in 1888 by George Routledge and Sons

Cataloguing in Publication Data
A catalogue record for this book is available from The British Library

ISBN 978 0 7123 5702 9

Typeset by IDSUK (DataConnection) Ltd
Printed in China

# INTRODUCTION

MIKE ASHLEY

The book you are holding is both rare and intriguing.

Until this republication it was almost impossible to locate a copy outside of the major research libraries. The online catalogue of all of the major UK libraries, COPAC, lists only five copies, though it's probable there are a few more held by dedicated collectors. The reason it is so rare is that the author, Leonard Merrick, apparently tried to buy up all of the copies he could find and destroyed them. Why? He never said, other than that he thought the book was terrible. It's not the first time that an author has come to dislike his first published book, for that's what it was, but it is unusual for them to go to the expense of buying as many copies as they can in order to destroy them. There has to be a reason, and I shall speculate on this shortly.

First published in 1888, this book is almost certainly the first ever British novel to feature a professional female detective. There were quite a few short stories about female detectives published during the middle of the nineteenth century. The British Library has republished two of the earliest such collections, *The Female Detective* by Andrew Forrester and the anonymous *Revelations of a Lady Detective*, most likely written by William Stephens Hayward. Both first appeared in 1864.

In the late 1860s the evolution of the detective novel as a distinct literary medium began to gather pace, starting in 1868 with the publication of *The Moonstone* by Wilkie Collins, featuring Sergeant Cuff. Other notable works include *Monsieur Lecoq* (1869) by Emile Gaboriau, with his eponymous police detective; *The Leavenworth Case* (1878) by the American writer Anna Katharine Green, with her police detective Ebenezer Gryce; and, most sensationally, *The Mystery of a Hansom Cab* (1886) by Fergus Hume, who was born in Britain but was then living in New Zealand. He had the book privately published in New Zealand, where it was ignored by one and all, but when it was reprinted in Britain it sold in its hundreds of thousands, becoming one of the bestselling crime novels of the period. Then came *A Study in Scarlet*, the first of the Sherlock Holmes adventures by Arthur Conan Doyle, published in *Beeton's Christmas Annual* for 1887 – and from then the detective novel really started to flourish.

But in all of these novels, and their lesser-known contemporaries, the detectives were men. So when in 1888 Leonard Merrick detailed the adventures of the unemployed twenty-eight-year-old Miriam Lea, after she responds to an advertisement by Mr Alfred Bazalgette's private detective agency, he was embarking upon the first full-length novel about a female detective.

Or was he? There are two possible forerunners that may challenge this claim, but we have to consider them carefully. One book often cited as featuring the first ever female detective is *Ruth the Betrayer; or, The Female Spy* by Edward Ellis, which was first serialized in weekly parts starting in February 1862. Ellis was the pseudonym of Charles H. Ross (1835–1897), though he sometimes wrote with a retinue of collaborators. He produced a mass of cheap penny dreadful and stage melodramas under several pen names and although he is almost forgotten today, the name of his best-known comic creation, Ally Sloper, at one time passed into the language. At the start of *Ruth the Betrayer*, she is actually called 'the female detective', by a policeman who whispers to a victim, 'she's a female detective – a sort of spy we use in the hanky-panky way when a man would be too clumsy.' But it is soon revealed that she is not a female detective at all, but is 'attached to a notorious Secret Intelligence Office, established by an ex-member of the police force.' The suggestion is that she is an undercover agent, at times an *agent provocateur*, but as the novel progresses it soon becomes evident that she's not really that either. She is her own agent, more than happy to use the police to her own ends to exact revenge on her enemies. Even her name is uncertain. Some call her Ruth Trail, but she's also known as Belinda Belvidere, a rich widow who runs a bawdy establishment. Whoever she is, she was not a detective, except when it suited her purpose to adopt such a guise.

The other forerunner to *Mr Bazalgette's Agent* is another matter entirely. The American equivalent of the penny dreadful was the dime novel: cheap fiction written for the masses, often serialised in story-papers and then issued in paperbound booklets with extremely small print. One of the most productive of the dime novelists was Harlan Page Halsey (1837–1898), who, in 1872, created the private detective Old Sleuth. The character became sufficiently popular for the publisher to release the *Old Sleuth Library*, which ran for twenty years from 1885 and was then recycled as *Old Sleuth Weekly*. Halsey wrote the original stories under the alias Tony Pastor, but soon the stories appeared as if told by Old Sleuth himself, narrating either his cases or those of fellow detectives, and other writers contributed to the series. One that Halsey almost certainly wrote was *The Lady Detective*, first published in 1880 and later reprinted under the title *The Great Bond Robbery; or, Tracked by a Female Detective*. This introduced Kate Goelet, a twenty-three-year-old woman of 'rare beauty and intelligence' who occasionally works for Captain Young, a former chief of the New York detective force but who now runs his own private agency.

Young employs Goelet to become acquainted with Henry Wilbur, who works for a New York bank and is known to have embezzled a million dollars. It is Young's belief that Wilbur is an innocent victim controlled by an unknown woman, and it is Goelet's task to pursue Wilbur, identify the 'siren' who controls him, and recover the stolen bonds, for which she will be rewarded with a fee of ten per cent of what she recovers.

There is no question that Goelet is a genuine detective and that she is almost certainly the first female detective in a novel-length story, albeit a dime novel.

Which brings us to Miriam Lea and *Mr Bazalgette's Agent*, which was published in July 1888, eight years after Halsey's *The Lady Detective*. Lea is taken on as a private detective by Mr Bazalgette's firm and her first task is to find a banker's clerk, Jasper Vining, who had previously forged financial documents which allowed him to acquire £40,000, and who has now absconded, with two bonds totalling £1,500. They do not know where Vining has gone, but suspect him to be somewhere in Europe. All that Miss Lea has to identify him is a year-old photograph. And so the pursuit begins.

On the surface it might seem that *Mr Bazalgette's Agent* could owe some debt to Halsey's dime novel, because they share not only a starting point but also, to some extent, an ending, which I shall not reveal here. However, these are the only points of similarity. Merrick's novel takes a totally different route from Halsey's. It is a much more light-hearted and less formulaic journey, taking us through a Europe with which Merrick was clearly familiar and leading on to South Africa, depicting the Kimberley diamond fields where Merrick had in fact worked between 1882 and 1885 as a superintendent of labour and where he had nearly died of typhus (which was then known as camp fever).

But could Merrick have read Halsey's *The Lady Detective*, and did he later feel some guilt over using that novel as the starting point of his first book and thus seek to destroy all copies? We will probably never know. Merrick's early years, according to his biographers William Baker and Jeanette Roberts Shumaker, in *Leonard Merrick: A Forgotten Novelist's Novelist* (2009) are 'clouded in obscurity'. He was born in Belsize Park, London in February 1864, and his surname was Miller. His father, William Miller, was a successful businessman who ensured that young Leonard had a first-class education, but when the boy was in his late teens his father lost money in a business venture and that was when, in 1882, he went to South Africa. He returned to London around 1885, changed his name to Merrick and became an actor, touring England, but he soon became disillusioned and turned to writing. After a few short stories he produced his first novel. *Mr Bazalgette's Agent* was neither critically nor commercially successful, so Merrick returned to the stage, this time in New York, but gainful employment was limited and he wrote a second novel which he discovered, when he returned to England, had proved a success. From then on he produced a stream of short stories, novels and plays to much critical acclaim. It seems he was admired by his fellow writers more than the public. No less than J. M. Barrie, the author of *Peter Pan*, called Merrick 'the novelist's novelist'.

Merrick never wrote another detective novel. Many of his books, such as *When Love Flies Out O' the Window* (1902) and *Conrad in Quest of His Youth* (1903), explore the tribulations of individuals trying to make their way in the world. Of particular interest is *The Worldings* (1900), which is strongly autobiographical and is a study of manipulation and deception. The novel concerns Maurice Blake, the overseer of a diamond mine in South Africa, who has a sufficient resemblance to his friend Phil Jardine that after Phil's death Maurice takes on Phil's identity with a view to inheriting the dead man's family fortune. Before arriving in South Africa, Maurice had travelled to both the United States and Australia. There is no evidence that Merrick did this, but the question hangs there. Did Merrick, or Leonard Miller as he then was, happen to read Halsey's *The Lady Detective*? Did the idea of that story stay with him so that when he turned to writing he used it, perhaps subconsciously, as the basis for his own first novel? And did he later regret that and therefore seek to destroy all copies?

It's an intriguing line of speculation, but perhaps, on balance, the question is academic. *Mr Bazalgette's Agent* is a far superior novel to *The Lady Detective*. Its writing and plotting are considerably more ingenious. It uses the diary form, which allows much to be hidden, relating events through the narrator's eyes rather than a third person's omniscience. The novel thus works as much on what is concealed as what is revealed. Even though it is a first novel it shows an unexpected sophistication and maturity, far removed from the brash crudeness of the American dime novel.

Merrick died in 1939, just a month before the outbreak of the Second World War. His first novel has been virtually unknown for over a century, yet *Mr Bazalgette's Agent* is well worth reviving, and should proudly claim the honour of being the first British detective novel to feature a professional female detective.

# MR BAZALGETTE'S AGENT

## CHAPTER I

*July 4th, 1887.*

A DREARY boarding-house sitting-room commanding a view, when the slatternly domestic chances to clean the windows, of an equally dismal London street.

The society usually met with, I imagine, in an establishment where a refined home and superior *cuisine* are advertised as procurable in a musical family at twenty-five shillings per week, and the inevitable landlady who assures you, *à propos* of nothing, she was "brought up to be a lady," evidently conscious you would never find it out.

The "musical family" has in this instance resolved itself into a red-haired child who murders "The Carnival of Venice" with the pertinacity of a barrel-organ deprived of its variety; and the society, to be explicit, consists of several young men who hurriedly depart after an early breakfast, two middle-aged females, and a valetudinarian who interests himself in floriculture, assiduously raising something impossible to determine, but presumably mustard-and-cress, against the wall in the backyard.

And these are my surroundings! For the time being, I am alone in the long bare apartment where Susan will presently come to lay the dinner. The *pièce de résistance* yesterday was beef, resistance indeed so strong that it defied your teeth; to-day therefore the *entrée* will be "curried mutton,"—otherwise beef, but *réchauffé* and rechristened.

Let me review my position! I have earned my living in the schoolroom and on the stage; that is to say, I was a governess until people discovered I had been an actress, and I was an actress till they discovered I could not act. What next? I have nothing to do; I am eight-and-twenty; and I own precisely four pounds thirteen and sixpence in the world. Three weeks more of the "refined home" to anticipate, and after that the deluge, with perhaps half-a-sovereign to buy an umbrella. Truly, Miss Lea, your prospects are brilliant!

And yet I believe I could smile at it all in other companionship; I fancy I could enjoy the present, and leave the future to take care of itself, if (detestable conjunction) there were only a present to enjoy. The sepulchral gloom of this *ménage* communicates itself and weighs me down in spite of my disposition; the ghastly silence and the faded respectability play havoc with my nervous system. Low spirits are as infectious as scarlet fever; and there is nothing upon earth more infectious than scarlet fever,—excepting a rich man's laugh!

I suppose it was dulness that drove me to these blank pages as a confidant, on the principle on which we always seek a friend, to share our sorrows, not to divide our joys. This, by-the-bye, suggests that if there were no trouble in life there would be no friendship either; how unflattering a reflection for humanity!

Nevertheless I know that to commence a diary is a mistake; I feel it while I yield to the temptation. It permits you, that fatal volume, to write all the spiteful things you must not say; and once begin to make spiteful comments on your neighbours, and you tacitly admit your own life to be a failure. Mine is to be a success. Yes, future repository of all my peccadilloes, I am not forgetting I shall be thirty in two years; I am painfully aware that unless something unforeseen turns up before the end of the month I shall bid Mrs. Everett's select circle a reluctant adieu at the express recommendation of my physician to try the South of France; and notwithstanding, I repeat it emphatically,—my life shall be a success! How? I wonder!—Goodness, what a fool I am, and here is Susan with the cloth!

\*          \*          \*          \*          \*

*July 7th.*

When I penned the foregoing entry three days ago, I was idealess; to-night, on the contrary, I am revolving a suggestion so positively original, that for the moment it deprived me of breath. The credit of this achievement belongs to a Mr. Claussen, perhaps the only man in the house with whom my conversation has extended further than admitting it was a fine morning, or saying "thank you" for the salt.

He is a clerk in an insurance broker's office somewhere in the City, and being a foreigner contrasts to advantage, socially, with the other residents, Messrs. Smith, Brown, and Robinson,—also clerks, but British ones. This evening he came upon me as I was studying the "*wanted*" sheet of the newspaper, and, to my own astonishment, I presently found myself explaining

a good deal more of my circumstances than was necessary, even going so far as to hint that an occupation
would not be totally undesirable.

"'Everything comes to him who knows how to wait,'
does not the proverb tell us?" he remarked in English.
"Ach, but that is a proverb so little understood. He *has*
to know *how* to wait, and by the time he has learnt,
the knowledge is of trifling personal use; he is too
old, yes?"

"Precisely," I returned, "waiting in an armchair, for
instance, is scarcely the advice intended?"

"Ha, ha, you see my meaning, you have perception!"

"Some while ago one of our periodicals published
a series of articles informing people how to live on a
pound a week; an interesting sequel would be 'How
to make it.' The instruction does not go so far as that,
however," I observed, "yet I wonder of how many
thousand lives it is the chief, the only study!"

"But," said Mr. Claussen, "you are a lady of brains, of
education——"

"And," I added boldly, "I am looking here to ascertain their marketable price!"

"So, so! Nevertheless, my dear Miss, you are wrong;
for it is not to this page, I would say to such a woman,
she should look!"

He laid a squat forefinger contemptuously upon it as he spoke, completely filling a vacant situation!

"No," he repeated, "not there!"

"'Not there, not there, my child!' Where then, Mr. Claussen?"

"Turn to the last sheet, my dear Miss; to the back of the paper instead!"

"You don't mean the 'Agony Column'?"

"Yes," he exclaimed, "you have it now! Certainly it has occurred to me that a woman of the world, a woman of appearance, of capacity, with whom, you follow me, the path is not of rosebuds, might glance there with advantage! *Es ist nur ein Einfall,* but it has been my thought! Here is a business where breeding must be a recommendation; do they pay for breeding in the linen-draper's shop? Here is a work where beauty is a passport; it is no passport to the schoolmistress, not at all. I am right, yes? Look!"

I did look, and this is what I read:

"ALFRED BAZALGETTE, 7, Queen's Row, High Holborn.—Suspected persons watched for divorce, and private matters investigated with secrecy and despatch. Agents of both sexes. Consultations free."

# CHAPTER II

*July 8th.*

I PASSED a bad night; perhaps it was only to be expected. At four A.M. I told myself even to have considered such a vocation was preposterous; at five I decided that, should the weather be fine after breakfast, I ought at least to obtain particulars; and then I grew alarmed again, and prayed it might be wet. It having rained persistently for three weeks the compromise calmed me, and I finally fell asleep.

Alas, the "mocking sunshine," as the poets have it, deprived me of my last hope when Susan called me some three hours later. So at noon, while the redheaded prodigy is belabouring the piano, behold me descending Mrs. Everett's front-door steps, with "my courage in two hands."

Praised be the saints, the sweet mama of the latest little terror I tried to teach had a Parisian maid; beneficent powers be also praised, I lent Félise French novels, and in return she made my dresses! I am reminded of the fact as I contemplate my reflection in a plate-glass window, the hang of my skirt, coupled with the consciousness of having expended I am ashamed to

chronicle *how* much a yard for the material, impart-
ing an exhilarating certitude about my costume. Yes,
Félise; you had your weaknesses, notably a *penchant*
for Zola, cigarettes, and the footmen, the last of which
predilections cost you your place; but with this your
creation on my back I am charitably disposed, and my
recollection is not a harsh one!

In Oxford Street I turned, and bought a pair of
gloves, declining "Our Reliable Chevrette" with the
delicate scorn of a millionaire, and disbursing four and
sixpence though my heart ached. I have not sojourned
eight-and-twenty years in this vale of tears without
discovering that the less you look in want of the thing
you solicit the more likely you are to get it. My toilette
being now calculated to inspire respect I proceeded
towards my destination.

No. 7, Queen's Row, High Holborn, was conspicuous only by a highly polished brass-plate bearing the
terse inscription—

"A. Bazalgette: Detective." On the right of the
passage in entering I found the name again, painted
in black capitals on a white background, "Second
Floor:—Bazalgette. Mendes.," and to the second
floor I nervously mounted. I was admitted to a small
front-room, in which I took a seat, amusing myself,

while waiting, by the perusal of a printed notice to the following effect.

"Detectives are to present themselves daily at 11 A.M.—All detectives to give voucher to Superintendent for sums received."

The announcement had a mysterious fascination for me, and I was gazing at it still when an individual appeared who politely inquired my errand. He was a negative sort of man, inclined to stoutness, who might have been any age from twenty-five to forty. His hair was sandy, his very freckles were sandy; he was sandy from his suggestion of whisker to the colour of his clothes; his cheeks alone discarded the prevailing tint, and they were florid and fat. You took him for the most simple, ingenuous of creatures until you met his eyes, and then you started, they were so bright and cunning. It seemed as if all the wickedness of the human race must be known to the owner of those eyes, and there could be no mortal depravity so uncommonly vile as to surprise him.

I said, "Is Mr. Bazalgette in?" And he replied, with the slightest tinge of foreign accent, "No, madam; is it anything I can do for you? I am Mr. Bazalgette's partner."

"You employ women, do you not?" I resumed diffidently. "I was led to imagine so!"

"Occasionally, yes: it depends on the business!"

"I ——, that is, what arrangements have to be made?"

"I can't tell you that without knowing what you refer to;" he smiled, "of course if you will explain your case you may be sure we shall adopt the proper measures."

"You misunderstand me. I have no case to confide. I learnt that you—er—did make such engagements, and being through reverses of fortune compelled to adopt some mode of livelihood——," I began desperately, and then stopped suddenly short for the overwhelming reason that I saw the man did not believe me.

"Well, come now," he said indulgently, "are you in trouble, or is a friend of yours in trouble, which is it?"

If at that moment the Brussels carpet could have yawned at my feet, and engulfed me, I am confident my sensation would have been one of unmixed gratitude. To be regarded by this cheerful wretch as a possible forger, or worse, scattered the last remnants of my self-possession, and sent the blood tingling into my face and neck with all the forty-horse blushing power of an *ingénue* in book muslin.

"Let us comprehend each other, Mr. Mendes, please, for I presume I am speaking to that gentleman!" I said as steadily as I could manage. "I have, as I stated, called to ask for employment on your staff; have you a vacancy, or have you not?"

For an instant, to do him justice, he evinced signs of being faintly disconcerted; then, "What are your qualifications?" he demanded.

"I speak French, German, and Italian; I have a tolerable acquaintance with the Continent, and—"

"Yes, yes! why do you choose this work?"

"Because I want money; moreover, because I think I have some latent aptitude for it."

"What are your references?"

"Are references essential?"

"Indispensable! We must always be certain there has never been anything against the applicant."

"I can furnish you with a testimonial from a lady with whom I lived in the capacity of governess, I brought it with me in the event of such a thing being required. It is, as you will perceive, dated ten months back, but I can assure you I have not committed a burglary in the meantime, and in it you can see for yourself the reason of my quitting her house.

"'Lady Edward Jones having ascertained Miss Lea has occupied a position on the public stage, and being unwilling that Master Pelham Jones should imbibe any vulgar tendencies towards art, will have no alternative but to dispense with Miss Lea's services at the expiration of the present quarter.'"

Apparently unable to appreciate the subtle loveliness of the extract I had quoted, Mr. Mendes read this precious epistle from the address to the final full stop.

"How have you lived since, Miss Lea?"

"On my savings; the exposure of my terrible past did not occur until I had been fulfilling my duties for two years."

"Ah; and you are staying now——?"

"Where I have been staying ever since;" and I gave him the number of the street.

I deemed it now time to put a few queries on my own account.

"Might I ask what salary you usually allow?"

"We have no fixed figure, it varies; we discharge all expenses, and pay *per diem* in accordance with the nature of the undertaking, from five shillings to——, well, we have paid so much as four pounds."

"A day?"

"A day."

Good heavens, twenty-eight pounds a week! It seemed incredible that a single member of the establishment should be remunerated at so vast a rate till I reflected the client would probably be charged double the amount in the bill.

"I need not tell you," he continued, "that was in extremely rare cases, and in taking fresh persons we try them on very small jobs."

"I should have thought," I remarked with emphasis, "a *lady* would have been valuable from the first; I have understood that Scotland Yard will pay any amount for ladies and gentlemen, they are so difficult to secure, and still more difficult to keep!"

I had not understood anything of the kind, but it was a venture, and it told.

"Of course," he rejoined blandly, "we do not get many applicants quite like yourself, but then it is seldom we should want them; our principal investigations are for divorce, and we send out our female agents most usually as ladies'-maids. Still, as you observe, there are exceptions, and occasions where——"

"Where a knowledge of the Queen's English and the usages of society are desirable! Well, what is your reply?"

At this juncture we were interrupted by the advent of a tall military-looking man with a springy walk, moustache-points fiercely waxed, and a brilliant silk hat set jauntily on the side of his head. Mr. Mendes glanced round at him, and nodded.

"How are you?" he said. "Will you go through?"

The new-comer strode into the adjoining apartment, through which I caught a glimpse of yet another door, but his arrival had terminated my interview.

"What is your reply, Mr. Mendes?" I repeated.

"We have no opening at present," he averred hurriedly. "Should an occasion crop up we will see! Now I must say 'good morning,' madam. If you are passing you might drop in in the course of a week or two,— good day!"

And so ended my wild attempt towards this strange career.

## CHAPTER III

*July 19th.*

ELEVEN days have passed; two pounds ten of my capital have gone to swell Mrs. Everett's exchequer, and on settling the account yesterday morning I gave her a week's notice, the next presented being the last I can defray.

I am in trouble about my trunk too. It would doubtless look remarkable to leave it in her charge; people
ordered abroad for the benefit of their health usually take
their portmanteaux with them. But though with strict
economy I shall have enough for a cab-fare on Monday,
and can depart in orthodox style, if I am hampered by
luggage, where on earth am I to tell the man to drive?
Without it I might alter my mind on the subject of the
previous direction delivered with great distinctness for
the benefit of Susan; get out; and complacently discharge
him well inside the shilling radius. I wonder if the cloak-
room at Charing-Cross ——, no, I suppose not!

Oh, "dere diry," I no longer feel the capability of
smiling if I had the provocation! Baggage apart, what
is to become of me, homeless in this wilderness of
houses? where am I going when I have shaken the dust
of Mrs. Everett's Kidderminster from my feet? For ten
months, with a roof to cover me, I have endeavoured
to obtain an occupation, and in vain; how then can
I hope to find one without a shelter, and deprived of
food? It is too terrible; in my most ultramarine fits of
abject depression, promoted by a protracted presence
of the two middle-aged females, I never imagined a
strait like this! It seems as if it could not be real, and yet
I know it is. Once, if another woman like myself had

told me she had tried during ten months in London to get employment and failed, I would not have credited it, or I should have said, "My dear little simpleton, you have not set properly about it!" Now from personal experience I learn how very easy of occurrence such a thing may be. Since I opened you last, my blotted volume, I have made a succession of visits to all the agencies whose books are adorned with the cognomen of "Miriam Lea"; I have spent sixpence replying to three bogus advertisements, and ineffectively walked myself tired to answer some genuine ones. Kismet! Unhappily the sentiment is philosophical but not filling, and one cannot live on philosophy,—unless, indeed, a publisher chances to appreciate it too.

On consideration, my sole resource is to secure the cheapest bedroom available; quit the Board and Residence accompanied by my belongings, and start pledging my wardrobe without delay.

And when it is gone?—I give it up!

\*          \*          \*          \*          \*

*July 21st.*

In pursuit of more ordinary avocations I had lost sight of Mr. Mendes' permission to return. Only

three more days remain to me; it is my last chance;
I will go.

*          *          *          *          *

*July 22nd.*

I am engaged! My hand is trembling so I can hardly
hold the pen. When I went in, Mr. Mendes was
exchanging some muttered confidence with a portly
personage I intuitively guessed to be his partner.
I did not devote much attention to the latter, however;
I only remember he struck me as being considerably
the elder of the two. My previous acquaintance recog-
nised me with what appeared to me a slight indication
of astonishment, at which Mr. Bazalgette raised his
brows interrogatively, and Mr. Mendes affirmatively
closed his eyes. From these rapid signals in woman's
own deaf and dumb language I gathered I had been the
subject of their conversation, and had not inoppor-
tunely arrived. After a few preliminary observations
my suspicion was confirmed.

"I have been talking of you to Mr. Bazalgette, Miss
Lea," said the younger man hesitatingly. "Indeed we
thought it possible we might communicate with
you."

"Indeed?" I remarked.

"You still believe yourself capable of conducting a negotiation?"

"Decidedly."

"Hem!"

"You are a linguist, I hear?" said Mr. Bazalgette, speaking for the first time.

"I know German, French, and Italian, yes!" I answered.

"And can converse in them fluently if need be?"

"In French as fluently as in English, I lived many years in Brussels; in German and Italian not with equal facility, but well!"

"You have accomplishments,—do music on occasion, eh?"

"I play and sing."

"So; come in here, Miss Lea, sit down!"

They preceded me into the inner office, which I found larger and much better furnished than the other, and I augured well from the invitation. Mr. Mendes seated himself at a mahogany desk confronting me where I lay back in the morocco leather arm-chair; while Mr. Bazalgette stood on the same side with his back to the empty grate, staring at me also.

I was beginning to feel queer.

"Now, Miss Lea," resumed the former of the pair, if we should consent to intrust a commission to your charge, not a job of following a suspected person on foot or in cabs, but with a really big case, are you willing to undertake it?"

"Yes."

"I think so!" said Mr. Bazalgette dreamily, as if he had been asked a question too.

"Then listen, and when there is anything you don't understand have it made clear! Mr. Bazalgette's services have been solicited by Messrs. Wynn, May, Reimer and Company, the financiers of Lombard Street, to trace an absconded party. Perhaps you have seen some particulars of the affair in the papers? The man we want is their late managing clerk, Jasper Vining. On the eighteenth of April this person pleading extreme ill-health sent in his resignation, ostensibly intending a lengthy sojourn in Australia. That there was any motive beyond the explanation he tendered was not suspected, for, although it is now ascertained he was accustomed to plunge heavily at cards and on the turf, he comes of a first-rate family, and had for years enjoyed the entire confidence of the House. His resignation at a month's notice was therefore a subject for regret; all the same they parted on the best of terms.

"After his departure, not till a month after, for he had planned his *coup* well, it transpired that during the four weeks previous to April the eighteenth he had been systematically forging bills upon the firm's correspondents in Vienna, Berlin, St. Petersburg, and Copenhagen to the tune of forty thousand pounds; in his capacity of manager, himself opening the letters containing the forged bills accepted, and subsequently discounting them on the Exchange. Besides this, taking with him in his flight one one-thousand, and one five-hundred-pound bond of Egyptian Unified Loan which had shortly before come into his possession in the ordinary course of his duties connected with the Stock-Exchange Settlement. Is it plain to you so far?"

"Quite, thank you; will you go on, please?"

"Messrs. Wynn, May, Reimer and Company's first step on discovering the fraud," continued the detective, "was to immediately consign the matter to the dexterity of Scotland Yard, whose efforts, as yet, have *not* been crowned by success. The time has certainly been short, but the interested parties growing impatient have now very naturally come to US."

If the "not" had been uttered in italics, the "us" was delivered in capitals. No type in Printing House

Square, however, could have rendered entire justice to the pronoun as it was pronounced just then by Mr. Mendes.

"And now, Miss Lea," he concluded impressively after the briefest pause, "I must inform you Mr. Bazalgette, with the most signal mark of esteem, has decided to confide the necessary operations in this affair to you!"

"I am grateful for the opening! And those operations will be——?"

"First to find the man; then to be in his company till you have got sufficient information to convince the authorities you have a right to demand an arrest! That you may appreciate how exceptionally fortunate a young lady you are," insisted Mr. Mendes, who did not appear able to lose sight of the fact, "I may tell you that, in the whole course of his experience, Mr. Bazalgette only remembers two cases where important business like this has been committed to raw hands, and then the possession of social polish in the agents was not merely desirable, but absolutely indispensable!"

"I shall endeavour to justify Mr. Bazalgette's confidence," I returned sweetly, "and yours too, Mr. Mendes. But on the subject of the arrest:—how am I to make it if he resists?"

"*You* do not make the arrest at all, it is a Treasury prosecution; simply communicate with us!"

"And I suppose I am to search for him anywhere but in Australia?"

"Exactly; he may be in any country but the one he gave out he was going to,—although, I don't know! He is smart enough to choose that very one in preference to all others!"

"I think not!" said Mr. Bazalgette, opening his mouth again. "He would never risk a destination where he could not arrive until after the exposure in England had taken place; the voyage to Australia is too long. Regarding the Continent, a swell like Jasper Vining lives in capitals or big cities, and it must be borne in mind he was personally known to those correspondents of his firm on whom he drew the forged bills; therefore, unless we except Hamburg as a probable refuge for a bachelor, we may also dismiss Austria, Russia, Denmark, and Germany!"

He accompanied his calculation by a rapid motion of his forefinger, as if he were actually demolishing the countries he named; indeed, under the guidance of this wonderful man, the map of Europe seemed to be dwindling to half its natural size.

"We do except Hamburg?" inquired his partner. "H-u-m-ph,—yes;" he rejoined, "you will go to Hamburg first,

Miss Lea! In all towns you visit under our instructions you will stop at the best hotels, and wherever it is practicable, obtain lists of the recent arrivals."

"And if I see his name how am I to act?"

"You are not expecting him to travel as Jasper Vining, are you? The name will of course be an assumed one, but it must be amongst the recent arrivals you make investigations. Do you follow me?"

"Yes."

"Here," and he drew out a capacious portfolio, "is the party's photo; it was taken a year ago, and given by Vining to Mr. and Mrs. May. He is handsome, well-made, and about forty years of age. You will have this with you for purposes of identification, but be prepared for some alteration of appearance, the loss of the moustache, the growth of a beard, or such like! Every day you will send us a report of your movements; in no case will you leave a city without authority, unless upon sudden and most urgent occasion. Here is a cipher, and here the 'key;' in the event of wiring the cipher is to be used. See if you understand it!"

"It looks perfectly intelligible,—yes!"

"The telegraphic address is 'Bazalgette, London;' letters you will direct to 'A. Bazalgette, Esquire, 7, Queen's Row, High Holborn,' don't say 'Detective!' Write that down—here is a new note-book; and put the likeness, and the cipher, and the 'key' in the pocket of the cover. You had better call yourself a widow— *Mrs.* Lea; good name, 'Lea,' eh? nothing conspicuous about it?"

Mr. Mendes signified approval.

"As a lady you will travel with your own maid."

"Where shall I engage her, in London?"

"She will be provided; one of our female agents will go with you in that capacity."

"I am to be under surveillance?"

"There is no question of 'surveillance' about it. The conduct of the affair is in our charge, and the finer portion of the actual work in yours, but it is perfectly impossible that you could go alone, and this woman's knowledge of the rougher part of the business you will doubtless find useful! Now, is there anything further you want to know?"

"Yes;" I said, "to go to the best hotels as you instruct I shall require several different toilettes, which I don't possess; walking costumes, dinner dresses, etc."

"Can you manage on fifty pounds?"

"Pretty well."

"Very good, then; you shall have the money."

He wrote a cheque for the amount suggested, and passed it to Mr. Mendes, with the request that he would see it cashed at once.

"I should like to know, too, what salary you propose to offer; also, if out of my salary I am to pay the bills and railway fares?"

"All expenses we defray," he responded; "your salary will be—a pound a day. Is that satisfactory?"

"No," I demurred calmly, "it isn't! I am not prepared to quit my home and friends, to be, pardon the word, ostracized by society for a pound a day."

"I think you exaggerate," he remonstrated. "Because you enter our employ you would hardly be an ostracite!"

"No, I am quite sure of that!" I answered, and I nearly laughed aloud at his mistake. "But you must admit I should be renouncing a good deal for a temporary occupation very poorly paid. When I was here before, Mr. Mendes asserted you seldom required the services of a lady; so that, on the termination of this undertaking, I should be without an engagement from you, probably find it extremely difficult to return to more ordinary occupations, and only have earned a trifling sum to make amends for the embarrassment. No, Mr. Bazalgette," and I inspected the tips of the four-and-sixpenny gloves with gentle regret, "if that is your proposal, I am sorry, but I must decline!"

"We might go so far as thirty shillings, I can't offer more! Do you agree or not?"

I dared not venture losing ten guineas a week by stipulating for still higher payment, so bowed assent as Mr. Mendes re-entered the room.

"Then that is settled! Kindly affix your signature to this contract, Miss Lea, and to a receipt for that fifty pounds. To-day is Friday,—you will present yourself here to-morrow, be ready to leave London on Monday, and a hundred pounds for expenses will be placed in your hands on that morning. Now, good afternoon!"

\*          \*          \*          \*          \*

*July 25th.*

I CAN only make a brief note, but I feel this portentous day should not be allowed to pass without an entry of some sort. At twelve o'clock I was with Messrs. Bazalgette and Mendes in their office; at five my costumes came home, not bad considering they were ordered barely four days ago, and that yesterday was Sunday; at half past seven I bade adieu to the boarding house, though I did not deem it essential to inform Mr. Claussen I had ever acted on his suggestion, and shortly after eight I met Emma Dunstan at Holborn Viaduct.

I found her on our introduction a hard-featured woman of modest demeanour, quietly dressed in black. I address her by her surname, and she calls me "ma'am." I had wondered whether she would when we were off the stage, I mean when we were not acting; but she did it as a matter of course, and I suppose there are degrees even among policemen. She occupies the second-class compartment behind me now, and I, in well-padded and uninterrupted privacy, am scribbling this in the train between London and Queenborough, *en route* for Hamburg.

I am not sorry to be alone, though my thoughts are none of the pleasantest company. Mrs. Everett's face appeared, or rather disappeared, like the countenance of a friend as I saw it last from the window of the four-wheeler; the dismal habitation where I have been bored so, assumed the proportions of a lost haven of refuge when once it was forsaken, and, oh, that sinking sensation of the heart as I rattled away through the gaslit streets to the station, and realised the nature of the mission on which I am engaged.

The enormousness of the operation struck home to me then with full force. Deprived of Mr. Bazalgette's reassuring presence, the magnitude of this pin-in-a-haystack search for a man I have never seen, frightened and appalled me. And all the while beating its chilling sense into my brain, till I dreaded to find myself unconsciously repeating it aloud, was one sentence, one paramount thought:—"I am a detective!"

## CHAPTER IV

HAMBURG, *July 29th.*

I ARRIVED at ten o'clock at night three days ago, and am quartered with "my maid" at the Hamburger Hof. Opposite me as I write is the Alster Bassin, with ridiculously small steamers on it, like penny toys puffing up and down. It is four P.M., and the entire population appears to have chosen the *Allée* before my windows for their promenade.

I explained to the *portier* that I had reason to believe a letter from my cousin had miscarried, and was anxious to ascertain if she had reached Hamburg without my knowledge. A two-mark piece, and a smile, made him my devoted slave, and yesterday morning he presented himself to 'Madame Lea' with a file of the 'Hamburger Fremdenblatt' of the past six weeks, containing a list of all the arrivals in the town.

Deeming it just as well to prosecute my researches a short time further back, however, I called at Streitt's Hotel, as well as the hotels St. Petersburg and De l'Europe, and with the same excuse received permission in both instances to examine the 'Strangers' Book.' Having done this, I feel that I have been brilliant but not successful! To personally inspect all the Müllers and the Schultzes, and the Blancs and the Greys, who since the eighteenth of May last have been deposited in this bustling German port is beyond me. I can only attentively study Jasper Vining's photograph, and frequent the places of most public resort. I am going directly to the open-air concert at Uhlenhorst.

The work is not so bad as I had feared; there is an excitement about it, and you live like a lady; the only objection is you feel such an impostor when a nice woman is friendly with you. I have decidedly thrown away any chances of advancement I might otherwise have had, but the chances were not distinguishable, and *il faut vivre!*

How unevenly the world's goods are divided; and how useless making an elaborate arithmetical demonstration to a socialist that he would only be something three-farthings better off if the division were to occur all over again! It is like arguing with a starving wretch on the futility of craving for a single meal, because if it were given to him he would still be hungry in the morning.

Here I am in a profession (is it a profession, I wonder?—I daresay; it is called a profession to murder innocent men, why then should it not be one to detect the guilty!) Here I am on a mission which if they knew it would cause people to shrink away from me, and yet my offence is, that, after struggling to obtain a livelihood for the best part of a year in the greatest capital of modern civilization, I was absolutely forced to make myself an object of general abhorrence by the discreditable fact that circumstances were stronger than I! What a crime! Britannia rules the waves! She would be better occupied in finding food for the Britons!

But it was not to make cynical reflections in a diary that I was sent here by Messrs. Bazalgette and Mendes; I am going out!

\*　　　\*　　　\*　　　\*　　　\*

*August 9th.*

Hamburg, with all due deference to its manifold attractions, is, so far as I am concerned, a failure. I have more

than once braved the perils of a fifteen-minutes' voyage
to Uhlenhorst, where I was surprised at the excellence
of the music, until I heard the conductor's name; I have
sipped coffee at the square wooden tables of the gardens,
and, observing a faraway look in Dunstan's eyes, decided
it was occasioned by a recollection of 'appy 'ampstead.
I have worn out a pair of shoes on the Jungfernstieg,
and cultivated a taste for Wagner, but, alas, I have not
encountered Jasper Vining.

By-the-bye, the capabilities of my coadjutrix do not
tempt me into any gushing dissertations! Up to the
present all the luminous ideas have been mine, not hers.
It is true I have not set the Thames on fire, or (to throw
in a little local colour) I have not ignited the Elbe, but
the ideas have been luminous all the same.

You, my smudgy confidant, I admit have been
neglected, but I have not the time nor the patience to
keep a double diary, and my daily reports to London
recording my bills, walks, talks, and thoughts, are
detailed enough to satisfy a lady's confessor. They even
appear to satisfy my employers now I have grasped
the style of thing desired. At first it was objected
I digressed too much; the firm was not anxious to
learn I had been sleepy when we arrived at Flushing,
or to be favoured with my opinions on the German

scenery; but now that I comprehend the sort of particulars expected, and couch them in the telegraphic-
ally brief sentences of the French *feuilleton*, amiability
reigns supreme.

In my last I communicated the unfavourable result
of my investigations in this city, and by reply am bid-
den to depart for Spain and Portugal, visiting San
Sebastian, Barcelona, Seville, Madrid, and Lisbon in
turn. I leave at 10.5 to-morrow morning, and am due
in Cologne at seven the same night. Dunstan does the
packing. Fancy me with a maid!

*            *            *            *            *

PARIS, *August 11th.*

What a journey! I am stopping here the day, as there is
no express until twenty minutes past eight this evening.
Dunstan's fare from Cologne cost as much as mine,
only first-class compartments being available unless we
remained for the seven o'clock train next morning; as
it was we had to wait three hours and a half!

The waiter informing Madame it was but five minutes' walk to the Cathedral, we went to see it, and
Dunstan declared it was "'andsomer than the Brighton

Pavilion!" After that I discarded conversation for Galignani, and read it in the waitingroom.

Among petty trials is there one more odious than to view a sight which impresses you in unsympathetic company? The primary sensation is one of unmixed delight; the second, a feeling of dumb rage that is not reciprocated; and the third a keen annoyance that you have been moved yourself.

If Dunstan had been a lady I should have quarrelled with her. If *I* had *not* been a lady I should have shaken her! As it was I dissembled with the newspaper, and chafed till half-past ten. Paris looked delicious in the early sunshine as we drove from the station to the Grand, and after my night's sleep in the *wagon-lit* I was able to thoroughly enjoy my breakfast, for which, including *vin ordinaire* which I did not drink, I disbursed the comparatively modest sum of five francs.

My ideas on the subject of expenditure I notice are becoming regal!

I shall be glad when I have at length set foot in San Sebastian; as yet I have done nothing worthy to be mentioned, and, burning as I am to distinguish myself, it is aggravating to perceive my present entry closely resembling the absolute inanity of a guide-book!

\*     \*     \*     \*     \*

SAN SEBASTIAN, *August 14th.*

"I am here!" I believe that was somebody's motto; if it was anybody victorious I apologise, for though I came and I saw two days ago, the important climax of the Latin quotation would be inappropriate. I am domiciled at the Hôtel de Londres (called 'de Londres' presumably because, being like an immense villa in the middle of a garden, it immediately suggests Claridge's or the Langham), and under other conditions the place would amuse me. You have to grow accustomed, for instance, to only one woman in thirty wearing a bonnet, the majority of feminine head-gears being the *mantilla*; and it is a novelty to see fans esteemed an indispensable adjunct to walking costume in lieu of sunshades. Now that the first shock which these departures occasioned is beginning to wear off, however, I am forced to admit a couple of yards of black lace may, put on *à l'Espagnole*, make a very efficient substitute for the creations of Louise, and to sorrowfully acknowledge the language of the fan has been as utterly unknown to me as the language of the land; more so, indeed, for I found a strong resemblance between the latter and Italian.

But the fan, what do these women not make it say!

In the first place they carry it differently to us; in the second the wariest *chaperone* in Belgravia would be baffled by its capabilities for speech in the grasp of a Southern beauty of sixteen. "I like you," and "You bother me," "You may follow me," and "You are to wait here," are, I learn, among the commonest forms of expression in this most mysterious of tongues.

There are a mama and her two daughters staying in the Hotel; I say "mama" because the term describes her so much better than "mother." She is the typical British matron, and the condemnatory voice in which she talks about "these foreigners" is glorious. She scans them superciliously in the street through a *pince-nez* as if she were inspecting the serpents at the Zoo, and, I verily believe, regards their presence in their own country as an unwarrantable intrusion.

I made her acquaintance this morning, the fact of being English, and travelling with a maid, probably recommending me to her favour. A maid is a great credential, almost as "tone-y" as a hyphen, and "Mrs. Shoddy-Johnston's carriage blocks the way" sounds well, it is admitted, else why the connecting dash?

"So theatrical," she finds the attire, she informed me after entering into conversation as graciously as if I did not know she would cut me in Regent-street to-morrow if we met there, "so theatrical, isn't it? The sort of thing one expects on the stage, or at a fancy ball!"

I shivered in the most approved insular fashion, and agreed. Is it not my *rôle* to be on speaking terms with as many persons as possible wherever I may be?

"Quite so," I assented, "it is a terrible blow to one's taste; only the chimney-pot hats of our compatriots in a measure relieve the eye!"

Here the daughters, enthusiastic art-students, it transpired, flatly contradicted me with all the happy spontaneity of short skirts.

"They couldn't think that by any means," they cried in a duet, "the introduction of those conventional hats into the picture seemed an anachronism, fortunately they were rare! What, now, could be more charming than the type of face? Had I noticed the colouring?"

Conscious of the mendacity of my statement I temporized, and confessed the "colouring" had not been duly observed.

"We are going to get some of the peasants to sit to us," they continued, mollified. "Mama wouldn't have come if it had not been for us, but one does so much better work where one can select one's models, and sketch them from one's own point of view! Of course you know Weatherley's?"

No, I did not know Weatherley's, and they said, "Ah, we forgot; you see we are so used to the Art-world we take these matters quite for granted!"

I converted a laugh into a cough, and attempted to direct the discourse to more personal channels, inquiring after the English tourists.

"Oh, we see nobody, nobody at all; we are certain not to have met your friends (you did say 'friends'?) unless they are artists!"

"Well," I returned, "they happen to be! The friends I am hoping to meet are mostly singers and musicians!"

It was undeniably weak, for I was scarcely likely to derive any profitable information after this, but these children's assumption of superiority was beginning to irritate me.

"Musicians!" they echoed coldly. "Oh, but we meant artists, 'painters' perhaps you would call them, not,— not that sort of people!"

"Indeed, I used the designation in its wider sense!" I responded humbly, and as the map of Europe had appeared under the eliminating influence of Mr. Bazalgette to be swiftly shrinking before my eyes, so, during the remainder of the interview with the 'art students' did the Art-world gradually resolve itself into a territory devoted solely to palette and brush, and bounded by Weatherley's class-room and the 'National.'

Interesting as this little family group may be, it is plain its members will not advance me, so I drop them. The full difficulty of my undertaking grows upon me every hour, threatening at times the proportions of a Frankenstein till I quail before it in anticipation, and, analysing my emotions, I suppose I must have looked forward to my efforts being crowned with instantaneous results. Nevertheless I know it would be absurd to feel discouraged so soon, and, distant or near, success shall be mine yet. I will find Jasper Vining; *I will find him*, and when I do, if I fail to furnish a conclusive proof of my abilities in the shape of his arrest, may I——, may I end my days listening to Czerny's hundred-and-one exercises for eighteenpence an hour!

## CHAPTER V.

LISBON, *October the——*

WELL, horribly near November! I am not inditing a report, and I have a distinct aversion to "coming to figures."

This reservation, being interpreted, means I am ashamed to confess how long has passed since I opened my diary last; how long it is since the determination with which I perceive I penned the foregoing lines has been succeeded by an ever-increasing despair. Yes, it must be chronicled these leaves have been untouched for the humiliating cause that I have had nothing to say; I have not justified the confidence reposed in me, and my ardour is damped by the knowledge. While in Barcelona I had to ask for a further supply of money, the initial hundred pounds, beneath the claims of bills, railway-fares, and two weekly salaries, having melted with awe-inspiring rapidity.

It was remitted forthwith, indeed Mr. Bazalgette does not appear to regard my lack of success as despondently as I do myself. From what he terms his "advices" he seems to think I shall be extremely useful in making Jasper Vining's acquaintance when he is encountered, but that his discovery might be accelerated by the assistance of an "old hand," Anglicè, a practised detective who should travel with me as my brother, in place of Dunstan.

This suggestion I have respectfully but firmly declined; the Vicar of Daisies-on-the-Grass having full cognizance of the occupation to which I have lent myself, would, as it is, probably withhold an invitation to "drink tea" with his gentle offspring; but, the vicar's censure notwithstanding, I still retain sufficient *amour propre* to object to trapesing about Europe in the society of a strange man.

Dunstan, like port and the gentleman of the comic song immortalised by small boys in the London streets, improves with time; she is all right when you know her. She has favoured me with some reminiscences calculated, if publicly dispensed, to do away with the necessity for curling-tongs. If I ever had the chance of presiding over somebody's establishment, I should, I think, be inclined to eschew a *femme de chambre*. That is,—I mean,—of course, if I were not a model of all the domestic virtues!

"Dere diry," although it was only between you and me, I am still red over that very equivocal remark!

She tells me she is engaged to a young man in *our* profession, and on the last job (she calls it 'job') upon which she was employed, like Boisgobey and a female Gaboriau, they worked in collaboration. Her *fiancé's* mission was to drive a Hansom cab, taking precautions to be, under various disguises, crawling along—Gate at the times conveyed to him by her; so that without surmising it, the 'suspected person' was almost always driven by an agent of the detectives. How nice!

She is helping me in my search as much as she can, but avers that at this stage of the proceedings dexterity is less potent than luck. It sounds an unprofessional statement, but from experience I should say it was true. Nobody could have tried harder than I have, yet how far am I advanced? And I have the consolation of recognizing I may continue in a similar fashion for months. I feel myself developing into a sort of *Juive errante* without an eventual abiding-place; the whole length and breadth of the Continent may be traversed without bringing me relief! I pitch my tents in comfortable spots certainly (the dining-*salon* here is the handsomest I have ever been in), but the lurking sensation of excitement which was at first a stimulant has deteriorated into a perpetual uneasiness which prevents me being still. I have no *peace*; what a beautiful word that is, and under ordinary conditions how seldom the want of it seems needful! Why, at that wretched boarding-house at home, I could compose myself on the sofa, and forget my troubles in a book; I cannot do that now. Granting I have the leisure, the printed paragraphs dance up and down beneath my gaze, and swim stupidly away into the margin where sense refuses to follow. My sleep is broken, and my dreams are horrid. In a sentence, my temperament is altering. Does not Victor Duruy affirm that after changing man's surroundings for two or three generations you will have changed his constitution, his ideas, and his disposition as well? It has not taken three generations in this case, merely three months, perhaps because I am a woman. Good gracious, what a monstrously egotistical production a diary is! You are 'swellin' wisibly,' my manuscript, like the visitors at Mrs. Weller's tea-fight, and to think your contents are all about me! I wonder if I could have scribbled so much of any other kind of composition,—probably not; I suppose most human beings find it easiest to be fluent upon themselves!

I have been exchanging confidences with the waiter; *au pied de la lettre*, he was inclined to be communicative, so I let him talk. Like the majority of his compatriots in his own station, José has been on the staff of English and French restaurants besides the Portuguese, and his speech when he essays "English as she is spoke" is eccentric in consequence. He came up to me just now to inquire backwards:

"Madame will not go out to visit the Passeio Publico?"

"No, José, it is going to rain!"

"But madame does not go out in the fine! It will not rain!"

I am not to be worried into the Passeio Publico against my will, so I say crossly:

"I have a headache, José, that is all!"

At this the little man is genuinely concerned. "Shall he summon madame's maid?" he demands; "at least madame will permit him to draw the curtains of the apartment where madame gives herself the trouble to sit!"

After insisting on carrying out this 'remedy' he disappears, to seek Dunstan, it transpires, for he returns ten minutes later, much exhausted, with the intelligence that she is not in the hotel. Having dispatched her on an errand I was previously aware of the fact, but the kindness affects me all the same; affects me indeed to the extent of a gratuity at which the pathetic monkey-face beams rapture.

"Madame is too liberal, too good! It is the same with all the English!" (If I had been a Hottentot I daresay a similar national characteristic would have been discovered.) "Unlike his fellow countrymen, who mock themselves of one's distress, the English people are generous to exaggeration; otherwise how would a poor

*garçon* exist in the great London *cafés*, where he gets
no wages and must pay so much a day to be allowed to
serve!"

"All right, José, I am glad you are pleased,"
I rejoin.

"'Pleased'! He ecstasizes himself! Is it not again
the method of the English gentleman who stays at the
Hôtel Durand? Do not the beggars in the *Almada* call
him 'milor' solely on this account?"

"What is that José?" I ask with sudden interest.

"The English gentleman who flings always away the
silver pieces!"

"Oh," I say, "and how long has this millionaire been
here?"

"It is," he must pause to recollect, "perhaps six
months since he first came!"

I do a rapid mental calculation; Jasper Vining sent
in his resignation with a month's notice on April the
eighteenth; roughly, therefore, he left for his unknown
destination on the eighteenth of May. June, July,
August, September, October! It is six months all but
a fortnight! Why might this not be he? I can barely
command my voice as I continue:

"And what is his appearance, odiously ugly,
I suppose?"

"'Ugly,' not to think of it! He was tall, and of noble aspect!"

Hotter and hotter! My fingers begin to twitch.

"I must see this paragon," I exclaim; "handsome and generous too, the combination is irresistible!"

To verify José's statement will, he assures me, be the simplest thing in the world after dinner; in the daytime, however, "Milor" seldom stirs abroad. He undertakes, if I post myself according to his directions, I may obtain a full view of the object of my curiosity this very evening.

Can it be possible my efforts are at length on the verge of fulfilment? Scarcely, the information has been too casually come by to lead to great results! And yet,—why not? It is not in fiction alone that a hint from an unexpected source supplies the clue we have so elaborately sought in vain. I may be sanguine, I may be foolish, but my presentiments seldom mislead me, and I have an inward conviction now that I am at last on Jasper Vining's track!

$$* \quad * \quad * \quad * \quad *$$

The "Milor" has been pointed out to me, at a favourable moment,—he was removing his hat to wipe his forehead.

He is as bald as a badger, and eighty years of age! I am too disheartened to write another word.

José has just handed me a telegram; it is addressed:—

"Madame Lea,
Grand Hôtel Central,
Lisbon."

The cypher runs:—

"The man is by nature a gambler; go to Monte Carlo."

## CHAPTER VI

Grand Hôtel Central,
*October 29th.*

No, I have not gone to Monaco; more than that, I am not going; more than all, there is a very excellent reason why!

All day I superintended Dunstan's arrangements for our departure, feeling, after last night's disappointment, a moral and physical wreck. What did the position of bonnets matter to me! I sat at the edge of the sofa, and looked on simply to supply an impression of assistance. Get crushed? Let them—was not I crushed too!

The world, for me at least, was over; it no longer existed, it had crumbled away. It is astonishing how frequently the world does assume this Stilton-like quality when there is a tinge of the 'blue' mood about one's self!

"What will you travel in, ma'am?"

"I, oh anything," I returned apathetically; "the one hanging up!"

Reduced to black-and-white this question and reply look ambiguous, to raise the most mild objection; but though the word 'dress' was mentioned by neither woman it was perfectly understood by both.

"Then there is nothing but the embroidered muslin to be put in, and that will go on the tray!"

Dunstan's tone as she confronted me on her knees was complacent in the extreme. "Now, ma'am, let me fetch you something to eat?"

"I've no appetite! How can I be hungry after this awful, this grotesque failure? The man was as old as the hills, and I had never thought to ask that wretched José his age!"

"Ah, you're fresh at the business, ma'am," she responded consolingly; "we get lots of false scents like this! Why, I'll be bound Mr. Bazalgette didn't expect you to be no quicker than you've been!"

"'Than I've *been*!' You talk as if I had finally arrived at a result; Monte Carlo may be of as little good to us as everywhere else."

"And what then! The longer it takes, the better for Mr. Bazalgette, isn't it; won't he charge according to time?"

This was an unconsidered aspect of the matter, and brought comfort, for I had been frightening myself into anticipating my recall. "Do take something, ma'am," she persisted; "a plate of soup?"

Like Mrs. Dombey, however, I could not "make an effort," and decided upon waiting until the dinner-hour, succeeding during the interval under the soporific effect of a new novel in obtaining, what I sorely needed, a nap.

Shortly after six I descended to the *table d'hôte*, and having taken my seat, was in the act of helping myself to tournedos à la Rossini, when my attention was arrested by a man's profile a few places lower down on the opposite side. He was a stranger in the hotel, most probably a new arrival in the city, for I had never encountered him in my 'investigations,' but directly his countenance caught my eye, it possessed some unexplained familiarity. Yet, so oddly does our memory play us tricks, when he had turned his head, and presented me with a "front view," I was for several moments (to use an Americanism) unable to "fix" it.

It was the bearded face of a man who had *lived* every hour of his possibly forty years, with a dissatisfied, cynical expression upon it augmented by the droop of his brown moustache.

How did I know him? I had recourse to a patent method of procedure of mine under these circumstances which I usually find effectual; I, in fancy, attired him in every variety of masculine habiliment that occurred to me. I put him in a postman's uniform, and I did not identify him as any postman I had been used to see; I clothed him in railway garb, and he defied recognition as a railway official. Then, with a reminiscence of London, I measured him for a frock-coat, and it fitted so admirably it might have been the handiwork of Savile-row.

Simultaneously two senses were endowed with occult properties: I saw a likeness lying in my despatch-box upstairs, and I heard Mr. Bazalgette's voice saying "Be prepared for the growth of a beard!"

Had I become the dupe of my own eyesight; was this another fallacious hope to be shattered? Or was he sitting there, the absconded managing clerk of whom

I was in search, Jasper Vining, bored and tangible, divided from me only by five feet of table-cloth, and an *epergne?*

I have no recollection of what I ate *after* that; I may have taken caviare with olives, or powdered my ice with cayenne; I had one sole thought, to remove any room for doubt as speedily as I could, and to send a message to England rushing under the sea:—"J. V. is here!" The lights confused me; they seemed alternately to burn so low the apartment grew dark, and to blaze into such phenomenal brilliancy that I was dazzled. Still I kept my watch upon the stranger, longing and yet fearing for him to rise; he was amongst the last.

I had José at my side in a second:

"Is that gentleman staying in the hotel?" I whispered.

"No, madame, he came to dine here; I do not know where he stop!"

There was no time to lose then.

"Send my maid to me, José, will you, at once; and tell her to bring me a hat, I shall be going out!"

The object of my scrutiny was now lounging in the entrance hall, rolling a cigarette, and as fortune would have it, a waiter, with a salver full of glasses, hurrying behind him as I passed slowly in front, pushed his arm. The pouch dropped to the floor, coming in contact with me as it fell, and scattering the long shreds of tobacco over my velvet skirt.

He must apologise, though it was not his fault; French or English, I wondered breathlessly. "I beg your pardon," he exclaimed; "it was awfully clumsy of me; pray allow me to brush it off!"

English by all that was happy, and without a trace of foreign accent.

"Don't mention it; I think it was the waiter who was to blame, although it doesn't appear to have occurred to him!" I said smiling.

Would he continue the conversation, or let it die? He spoke again:

"What a lovely night, is it not?"

"Divine," I answered (always vary the adjective in response to a platitude about the weather). "On such a night one can hardly realise that all the horrors of fog are just commencing at home, or one would be more grateful to be abroad!"

"Just so,—that is, I suppose they are; of course it will be November soon, as you say we forget it!"

His native land did not seem a topic adapted to arouse his eloquence, so I shifted to more general ground.

"What a pretty town Lisbon is!" I remarked inconsequentially enough, "don't you find it so?"

"If you are not used to the style it's rather interesting; but, for myself, I've lived on the Continent for years at a stretch!"

He had been so ready to impart this piece of information that he presumably felt some sort of supplement to it essential, he added quickly:

"I haven't many acquaintances in London, and unless one has it is not lively!"

"So," I observed, "you escape that common malady of our compatriots abroad,—home-sickness!"

"'Home-sickness'!" he echoed with a little laugh, "don't you think, deprived of the varnish of sentiment, 'home-sickness' generally means being profoundly sick of the place you're in! Are you doing much sight-seeing, may I ask?"

"I went to St. Roque to visit the silver chapel. I was told everybody ought to go there; but so far from imbuing me with the proper devotional spirit, I found all the lapis lazuli and mosaics had the opposite effect of making me dreadfully covetous. After that I gave up sight-seeing in despair!" I returned lightly. And at this juncture we heard Dunstan inquiring for "Mrs. Lea" as a moment later she approached us with my hat, she herself ready to accompany me.

Now I could not invite this acquaintance of five minutes to come too, undesirable as it was that I should quit him for ever so brief a period at the present stage, nor could I evidently postpone an intended stroll for the pleasure of his society. Only one course remained: I said "Good evening," very amiably, "one must choose the breeze on the promenade in preference to the stifling atmosphere of a house!" and trusted to his following me.

It was a poor chance, remembering his experience, and the limited opportunity I had had of being nice, but I could not help myself.

Once outside, Dunstan laid her hand on my arm, and muttered "It's him!"

Never did ungrammatical asseveration fall more sweetly on a woman's ears.

"You recognise the original of the photograph?"

"I'd bet my life on it!"

The 'lady's maid' had vanished into air. We were no longer mistress and abigail, but two female police-agents on the right track.

"Look back!" I murmured.

"It's worked; he's coming out!"

"Then we'll take the first seat, and he'll join us."

The prophecy was fulfilled; he presently came saun-tering past, and interpreting my bow aright paused beside our bench. Being no boy, however, he spared me an involved demonstration that the meeting had been accidental, and was content to perceive he had not offended.

Dunstan, again the discreetest of servants, moved to the other end, so as to allow him the space next me, and before long we were chatting together as if we had been formally introduced.

Nevertheless, I wanted to ascertain his name, or his alias, as fortunately as he had done mine. "How we (we of John Bull's island) drop our conventionality as soon as we are safely across the Channel," I hazarded; "here you and I, who only spoke to each other half an hour ago, are talking as freely as it would have taken us months to talk if we had met at Morley's or the Métropole!"

The bait did not draw.

"Yes," he answered, "but you see in a city like London, a person is not an individual, he is only one of a throng! To use rather a vulgar exemplification of my meaning, the Londoner's bulk of humanity is so very vast, he rarely takes the trouble to sample it!"

"I see the idea," I rejoined; "perhaps that is what the poet meant when he wrote about the 'little look across the crowd,'—there is seldom time to have much more! Owen Meredith, was it not?"

"I'm not sure," he replied simply.

"Ah, of course not; men do not go in for poetry, do they?"

"Well, I can't say; personally I am not one of the lady-novelist's heroes who are too languid to read anything excepting an occasional French novel, but nevertheless, quote Béranger with singular appropriateness when it is required to give point to a paragraph. I have read poetry in my time, and enjoyed it!"

"You surprise me," I remarked satirically; "I imagined such frivolities as crewel-work and Tennyson were confined to us! How chilly it has grown!"

"Chilly," he cried, "are you indeed!"

"Yes, the wind has changed, I fancy; I wish my maid had brought a wrap!"

"You should walk about for a while," he advised; "it is only keeping in one position."

"Whatever the cause may be the effect is decidedly unpleasant; and look, it is beginning to rain!"

It was indeed, I rejoiced to note! Two great drops had already splashed upon the gravel at our feet, and the skies were lowering.

"Oh, Dunstan, why didn't you bring my woolly!" I exclaimed reproachfully. "You know how easily I take cold; I have nothing to protect my throat!"

"Allow me to supply the deficiency as well as I can?" suggested our companion. "Let me lend you this handkerchief; it will be better than nothing. We are only ten minutes from your hotel!"

At last!

"Oh, thank you," I murmured, "thank you extremely if I shan't be robbing you! But how shall I send it back? I won't hear of taking you out of your way; it promises a regular downpour, and you are not staying at the Central, I think?"

"No," he replied nonchalantly, "I merely dined there this evening for a change; pray don't trouble to send it though! Keep it until we meet tomorrow; I may trust to be so fortunate I hope? Good night!"

"Good night, then, and thank you again!"

Delay for a needless instant was unendurable; no sooner had he left us than we sped homeward. Dunstan preceding me, I mounted the staircase to my room, hastily closed the door, and tore the handkerchief from my neck. It was of silk, and, as I had anticipated, it bore an embroidered monogram. Trembling with excitement I held the corner beneath the lamp; the initials were "J. V."——I have found my man!

## CHAPTER VII

GRAND HÔTEL CENTRAL,
*November 1st.*

IT is the third morning since the occurrence I recorded last.

The following afternoon I penned my daily report, containing on that occasion the communication of my discovery, and at six o'clock descended to the dining-*salon* devoutly wishing Jasper Vining might be there once more. In this particular I was doomed to be disappointed, though there was a mitigating circumstance in the shape of a pleasing item of intelligence imparted by José, from which I was able to ascertain the ingenious alias my prey has chosen.

This humble instrument of justice informed me the gentleman concerning whom I had inquired the night before, was, he had learnt *par hazard*, a visitor at the Hôtel de Bragança; he was a "Mr. Vane,"—"Jack Vane." "So far so good," I thought, as I subsequently reviewed the position of affairs whilst disrobing. "I now know his *nom de guerre* and his address!"

Therefore when I opened my eyes in the early sunshine yesterday, and saw Dunstan standing at my bedside with a cup of coffee, I felt at once I had awakened in the best of spirits. "He would naturally have allowed twenty-four hours to elapse before appearing here to reclaim his property," I told myself, "but to-day,—to-day, surely he would come." Yet, the briskness with which I made my toilette notwithstanding, yesterday was destined to prove one of the most perplexing and unsatisfactory of my life, for, in writing you up to date, my confidant, let me put it down without any circumlocution,—he did *not* come! No; on Saturday evening I parted from him on the Promenade; to-day, Tuesday, at 5 p.m., by the indisputable evidence of the clock in my own apartment, we have still not met again.

Now this is a great deal more than a blow to my vanity; it is a serious impediment to my plans. What is to be done? Let me think! There is one way: the handkerchief must be sent round to him with a polite acknowledgment of my obligation. This method of proceeding is certainly liable to suggest an undue curiosity on my part to have discovered what he omitted to state, his name and where he lodged, but I cannot afford to be hyper-delicate, and after so flattering an indication of the impression he has made on my susceptible heart, if I know anything of mankind he will dine here to-night beyond the shadow of a doubt.

"Dunstan," I exclaim, "take some tissue-paper out of a bonnet-box, and wrap up the handkerchief very neatly; then go round to the Hôtel de Bragança with it, and ask for our man, of course as 'Mr. Vane!'"

"Yes, ma'am," replies Dunstan, "what am I to say?"

"Say Mrs. Lea desired you to restore it, and to thank him exceedingly for the loan; that is all, but speak nicely, as if Mrs. Lea thought a lot of his lending it!"

"Yes'm!" And presently she departs.

Have I been wise, I speculate; will he leap at the conclusion I am an adventuress, and give me a wide berth, or (still more horrible contingency) under the idiotic belief, become so very conciliatory that I, on the contrary, shall be compelled to steer clear of him? It has been a bold move, but I remember Mr. Claussen's interpretation of "*Tout vient à lui qui sait attendre*," and decide I have done right!

I wonder if I may hope to gather any notion of what he intends from the account of my messenger. She has been long enough gone in all conscience; I waited an eternity before I permitted myself to look at the time.

Half-an-hour, three quarters of an hour loiter by, (they do not "pass," time never does when one is in a fever of impatience) and yet she does not return. One would imagine it was a *pilgrimage* to the Rua do Ferrejial! Can he be out, and is she remaining there to see him, or has she lost herself in a labyrinth of unfamiliar streets? I have just determined in favour of the latter explanation when the door is flung suddenly ajar, and Dunstan arrives.

Something in her face startles me; instinctively I feel she has important news.

"What is it?" I demand.

"I went to the hotel," she gasps, "and I asked for 'Mr. Vane!'"

"Yes,—well,—go on woman! Why, you have the handkerchief in your hand," I cry; "how's that?"

"Because 'Mr. Vane' sailed yesterday by the 'Grantully Castle' for the Cape!"

With this particular she sinks into a chair, and we gaze at one another in woe-begotten silence.

I rally with a forlorn idea.

"Then we must cable—somewhere, and have him taken when he lands!"

The stray crumb of consolation is denied me.

"Can't!" she says, "Only me and you know he's Vining; he's not been identified yet by any of the clerks or people who knew him in England, and I'll lay a wager Mr. Bazalgette reckons that necessary before we can get an arrest!"

*Bécasse*, simpleton, imbecile that I was, the man suspected me, and I had forgotten I was in a port!

"Perhaps one of the Lombard Street fellows is on the way out now!" she continues.

"The report of the discovery only went Sunday; it's not delivered yet!"

"So much the better!"

"Well, if we can't cable, what *are* we to do?" I moan.

Her answer is a terse one:

"Go after him!"

It seems to me correct as well.

"Make haste," I exclaim, "run downstairs, seize someone, the head-waiter, José, anybody, and find out when the next steamer goes."

And in the interval I march up and down from wall to wall in the manner of a frenzied Miss Trotwood, or a wild animal first caged.

In ten minutes Dunstan reappears accompanied by a sober functionary who has evident doubt about her sanity.

"There is no steamer for nearly a month," she ejaculates.

"Is that so?" I inquire anxiously of the official.

"Yes, madame; only the 'Castle' line puts in at Lisbon, the next will be the 'Pembroke Castle' on the twenty-eighth."

"Is there another line, then?"

"Certainly," he assures me in perfect English, "there is the 'Union.' The 'Union,' and the 'Castle' leave England on alternate weeks, but only the 'Castle' vessels touch here, and, of them, only one in every two."

It sounds like algebra.

"A Cape steamer of one sort or the other leaves London every week, if I understand you; are you sure of that?"

Yes, he is quite sure.

"Can you give me a 'Bradshaw'?"

The 'Bradshaw' is forthcoming, and three heads are simultaneously bent over its pages.

There is a train at half past eight this evening, November 1st. By dint of much study we ascertain that, taking it, we shall get to Madrid at 1.35 P.M. to-morrow; have five hours' 'wait' there; be in Paris early in the morning the day after, and (cry Dunstan and I triumphantly in a breath) reach London at 5.10 P.M. on the fourth.

"Pack, pack, pack. We'll do it together!"

We fling our things wildly into the trunks, dragging dresses from pegs, and shoes from under the toilet-table.

We have two hours fifteen minutes to do it all in. Surrounded by a pile of garments I pause for rest, and recollect I must wire our projected movement to Mr. Bazalgette. I ring the bell.

"Make out my bill, please," I request; "let me have a foreign telegraph form at once, and should any letters come for me after my departure, forward them to me in London at the Charing Cross Hotel."

"Yes, madame."

My throat is parched, and I feel as if I had not been to bed for a fortnight. I glance around; Dunstan's countenance resembles an exhausted chimney-sweep's.

"One moment," I add, "and send me up a pint bottle of champagne."

Two hours later we bid adieu to the Grand Central, bound for the Cape of Good Hope.

## CHAPTER VIII

ABOARD S.S. DRUMMOND CASTLE,
*November 26th.*

How long it is since I have made an entry! This though has been from no lack of leisure, but rather for dearth of incident, for what can be more monotonous than life aboard ship under conditions like mine! There is, however, my interview with Mr. Bazalgette which I have postponed recording.

I reached London at the hour I had calculated to behold it, and drove with Dunstan immediately to Queen's Row. I found the office open, and the partners within. They had naturally received the intelligence of Jasper Vining's presence in Lisbon, and were perplexed at the message announcing my return.

When I explained it, Mr. Bazalgette told me, more kindly than I had expected, that my general proceedings had been satisfactory, but had my experience been wider, I should have kept a more careful watch on the man when once he had been found. My departure with Dunstan for South Africa he viewed as a matter of course, she and I being, after the encounter, the most useful agents he could employ.

I asked him if her information had been authentic when she declared the arrest could not be procured without identification by someone to whom Vining had been personally known. He replied:—

"On the continent such confirmation would have been resorted to because it would have been the easiest form of testimony to lay before the authorities, who would demand what evidence was furnished beyond corresponding initials, and the resemblance to the photograph. But in the Cape this method would not be readily adopted owing to the distance; there what would be advisable after running him to earth would be to obtain proof of him possessing some portion of the property of which he had defrauded the firm."

"But," I remonstrated, "the property is money! You surely don't require me to swear to sovereigns; or to recognise bank-notes whose numbers the firm itself cannot know?"

"You forget," he spoke with the tolerance Richelieu or Machiavelli might have shown to the argument of a precocious schoolboy, "you forget Messrs. Wynn and Co. state he defrauded them of two bonds of Egyptian Unified Loan, one for a thousand, the other for five hundred pounds. Now, as far as such a thing *can* be ascertained, these bonds have not been disposed of; a cute man who meant to get rid of them would have done it without wasting an hour, and Vining is a cute man; what's the deduction? He holds them still, and having already made a haul of forty thousand, didn't reckon it good enough to risk being spotted for such a comparatively small affair as their sale!"

"Granted," I persisted; "admit he did not sell them, it does not follow he kept them!"

"A business-man does not destroy marketable stock!"

"Well then, he has them, but I can't rummage his boxes till I touch them with my fingers!"

"Now look here, Miss Lea" (it sounded quite funny to be called 'Miss' Lea again), "I do a great deal more with you than I do with many of my agents, I can tell you,—I give you my reasons! Listen to this: Vining is a gambler; if you had not met him when you did in Lisbon, you would have met him in a week's time, directly the season commenced, at Monte Carlo, I'd give odds on it; our ill-luck has been that you ran across him too soon, or too late, for in Monte Carlo he could hardly have escaped you so easily. That's past; what I mean now is that he'll gamble wherever he may be, and there is no question of forty thousand pounds in the hands of a man like him being esteemed the fortune it would be by you or I" (Mr. Bazalgette also shares the belief that "'I' is so much more genteel than 'me!'") "Suppose he is pressed for ready money, we don't want to wait so long if we can avoid it, but it's one chance, suppose he's short, what will he do then?"

The conclusion was obvious.

"The bonds!" I answered.

"Precisely," responded the detective; "and though I want to recover as large a part of the swag as possible, the chief thing I go for is to take the man himself!"

"Do you think, bearing his propensity in mind, he could have squandered so big a sum in six months?" I queried.

"I think," he retorted, "the Cape will help him, and when you do meet him you won't be troubled to stand by, and view him pitching Messrs. Wynn and Co.'s coin about long, for he won't have over much left!"

And after a week's delay in town through having reached England just one day too late for the "Trojan," it was with this not very brilliant prospect of success I resigned myself to braving a journey to South Africa.

I believe that is the right term; in books they always talk of "braving" a journey, as inevitably as they speak of the "good ship Twaddle ploughing the main," but anyhow it is correct in my case. It does require bravery to lie back calmly in a deckchair the whole long morning and weary afternoon when every nerve is strained in anticipation of arrival.

Bravery?—Well, say "Endurance!" The qualities are near akin, though the latter unreverenced word has to slink through the language associated with so far less pretentious a meaning;—definition probably due to the fact that men write dictionaries, and women endure!

I am beginning to hate this glittering expanse of sea without the relief of a sail. I am beginning to detest the evening refrains with which we are regularly enlivened (?) in the saloon; to lament the Bay of Biscay was ever created to lure weak tenors into warbling nautical ballads, and be sorry the nuisance of a "Midshipmite" was saved. If he had perished perhaps the "Cheery lads, yo ho," would not have made up a song about him!

Madeira was welcome: it took me out of myself (and the vessel) for a little while, since we went ashore in a party, and coming back, found the deck converted into a kind of temporary Lowther Arcade, and a swarm of tiny boats full of merchandise and boys bobbing alongside. It was amusing to see these curly-headed urchins, with eyes as marvellously blue as the waves, diving for six-pences, and re-appearing triumphantly with the rescued silver between their teeth. The island was picturesque, too; indeed, I secretly rejoiced the "Grantully Castle" had not touched there, and Vining could not have baffled me by making it his destination.

Alas, the variety was of brief duration, and presently we saw Madeira fade behind us (it ought to be "to something-ward," I expect, but I do not know what!), and once more returned to the tedium of maritime life.

Why is water so pleasant to hear in small quantities, and so depressing in large? I can listen to the splash of a fountain for hours; the roar of the ocean depresses me!

"Delightful," I have heard women say of some such voyage; "I was so sorry when we sighted land!" I wonder if they really were, or if the charm existed, like the fascination of one's school-days, in retrospection alone? From perception I am inclined to divide it into three parts: the first week, when each individual privately reflects how enjoyable the trip would be in different company; the second, when they have all grown sociable, and consider one another the most agreeable people they ever met; and the third, when everybody is inexpressibly tired of everybody else.

And how kind an interest the female passengers display to ascertain my reason for visiting the colony! Do men cross-examine their own sex so rudely?

Happily my explanation was invented before I came on board. I am a widow going out to see my younger sister and her husband, who will shortly join me in Cape Town. What an exposure if I left this lying about; nine "ladies" out of ten would read it before restoring it, with the casual remark that they had "picked it up below just two minutes since!"

*       *       *       *       *

Dunstan has been distinguishing herself; yesterday she saw a mouse in the cabin, and fainted. A good-looking steward happened to be near at the time to catch her. What a coincidence!

It seems he ran to fetch sherry, and, she tells me, "forced numberless glasses on her to bring her round." They will not be numberless when I get my wine bill, I daresay!

The other evening we were beguiled by a "Mock Trial" after dinner, a young gentleman with a lisp and a tow wig hastily manufactured (like his speech) impersonating the counsel for the prosecution. Funny if they played "Mock Trials" on the "Grantully Castle," Jasper Vining must have felt unwell!

Oh, that we were already on land! Every hour brings me nearer to him, and every hour he fills my thoughts.

I am sure Dunstan is not equally anxious, although she pretends she is; she will have to leave her steward, as she has already been parted from her *fiancé*, and how faithfully a plain woman does love——each time!

Besides, the matter after all is of much less importance to her than to me; it is I who will taste the sweetness of success or the bitterness of failure, and I do long to be successful! If I could only report, "You need not be inconvenienced to have him identified; you need be under no apprehension that the property is squandered; I have seen the missing bonds in his possession—cable next move!"

What a magnificent achievement it would be; should not I exult! And, apart from the honour, it would please me to do it for Mr. Bazalgette's sake, he has been nice to me. Oh, how I *yearn* for shore!!

\*     \*     \*     \*     \*

Joy! Table Mountain is in sight! The news spread round the breakfast-table like wildfire; porridge, chops, and buns were abandoned of one accord, and we all rushed on deck to strain our eyes at that very indeterminable object in the distance which appeared less like a mountain than a cloud.

It has been growing more distinct all the morning, and now we can make out some misty-looking spires around it, which the captain informs us are the Devil's Peak and Signal Hill; he says the commercial population will be staring up at the latter to learn the precise moment we get in. They cannot be more impatient for their mail than I am for their city!

I am too excited to watch with the others. I am scribbling this in my cabin, a deck one, and, see! Something like a vast stone barge laden with coloured porters and white hansoms is drifting past us. How strange! There is a perfect babel in my ears; a tumult of cries from all parts, everybody seems speaking at once. What can have happened? How silly I am; of course the stone thing is not moving at all, one would think I was a child! It is we who are floating by its side;—it's the wharf,—we've arrived,—thank Heaven!

## CHAPTER IX

St. George's Hotel,
Cape Town,
*(Three days later).*

This is my third evening here, and at the end of my second I found myself confronted with a serious difficulty; Vining was not staying beneath the same roof, and I could not call and inquire for him at the other hotels for fear the action should be reported to him, and he might elude me again. This obstacle necessitated consideration, but I finally hit upon a compromise.

It was highly improbable he would recollect Dunstan, weighing the fact that he only saw her once for a moment in the hall of the Central at Lisbon, and once in the dusk on the Promenade, where he certainly did not pay her much attention; so I have lent her one of my gowns, and she is going to have luncheon or dinner at all the principal hostelries, trusting to meet him thus. Let me find out where he lodges, without allowing him to suspect my proximity, and there is the first point gained.

Under my superintendence she made her toilette, and started this novel programme last night, but so far without avail; nevertheless it shall be continued, for there do not seem to be any restaurants here likely to tempt him out of doors with their *cuisine*.

What a capital it is, with its wide roads, and its dwarfed houses, and its niggers, and its Malays, and its solitary theatre! It is so old-fashioned it might be the city Cain built when he wandered forth after killing Abel, except that if it had been begun so long ago it must by now have presented a finished appearance.

I asked if many of the better people lived in the environs between Papendorp and Wynberg, and was told "Yes, nearly all the residents." I therefore hired a carriage, as being more suitable to our purpose than travelling by train, and drove along the high road, which at every mile or so has apparently been given a fresh name just to vary the monotony; no indication whatever of why Rosebank should leave off, and Rondebosch begin being visible.

I did not discern any inn of sufficient importance to make me deem it worth while alighting until we reached the extremity of all, Wynberg itself.

Here Dunstan and I descended, and, entering the porch, requested to be shown to a private-room, and provided with something to drink.

Lemonade-and-claret I opined nasty enough to be distinctly virtuous, so ordered that.

The proprietress brought it upstairs herself, and when I saw what a cheery, comfortable sort of woman she was, I repented I had not demanded ale.

"What a nice view you have!" I remarked encouragingly.

My experience on tour in the theatrical profession has taught me all landladies like to be complimented on their 'view,' if it only consists of oyster-shells and clothes'-lines.

"Do you find it so, ma'am?" she responded complacently. "It is mostly thought pretty; this time of year, of course, it's at its best!"

It sounded funny to hear of the country being at its loveliest a few weeks before Christmas, but it would not have done to say so, and thus admit I was a stranger in the colony. "Naturally," I replied, "I have often noticed your house, though I never came inside before, and have thought how charmingly situated it was! Indeed, a gentleman was questioning me about the prettiest spot round here, and I mentioned this, only the other day. Perhaps he may have come to you, a Mr.——, er, Mr.——; what *was* that gentleman's name, can you remember?"

"V——, V——," said Dunstan.

"I know, 'Vane!'" I exclaimed. "So, you see, without knowing you, perhaps I may have got you a lodger?"

"I'm sure it was very kind of you, ma'am, we've no 'Mr. Vane' staying here, but he may call; and much obliged to you I am! Won't you try a few biscuits with that?"

"Thank you, no," I returned, rising. "I am afraid we must be going now; good afternoon, we'll be certain to look in when we are passing next!"

"It was risky," Dunstan observed, when we were seated in the conveyance once more; "if you can go straight to work here, why can't you do it in the town too, ma'am?"

"Because I knew you would say 'V——, V——' first, and as soon as she didn't come out with 'Vane,' it was a foregone conclusion he was not there, before I uttered the name."

The drive back was pleasant. The sun was going down, and we could admire the scenery without having our appreciation affected by the heat. The fields where 'lilies blow' for nothing, and are crushed under foot as recklessly as though they would not cost a fortune in England, were observed and marvelled at. They grew so closely together, that the primary impression from our side of the hedge was of the ground being covered with snow. We also liked the effect (or I did) of a Kafir lying at the foot of a cactus, with a clump of maiden-hair fern for his pillow, and a golden cluster of bananas in the dust at his side. I wish I could paint!

To-night, in furtherance of our plan, Dunstan goes to dine at the Royal.

\*        \*        \*        \*        \*

*December 7th.*

News! This morning I said to Dunstan, "The 'hotel scheme' is a failure; we must conclude that although it did not strike us as probable, he is living in the suburbs!"

By-the-bye, we ascertained there was another one, Greenpoint, which we had also visited without success.

"Now," I continued, "I'll tell you what I mean to do; the people staying outside use the railway to come in, it isn't half an hour's journey. There are any number of trains running backwards and forwards; I shall go down to the station, and watch the arrivals and departures!"

Dunstan believed my plan might lead to results. Accordingly I sallied forth. In five minutes I was in Adderley Street; in five more I had reached the station. It was magnificent weather, and lots of people I found were loitering about the ticket-offices and doorways. I was pleased at this; in the crowd I fancied my prolonged stay would be unobserved.

I strolled with elaborate semblance of carelessness through the wooden barriers which stood open and unguarded, and ensconced myself in a corner of one of the seats. Here, if I am noticed, thought I, it will be supposed I am waiting for some acquaintances by appointment, and that they are late.

The occupation began to get tedious. I looked up at the clock; twenty minutes had passed, and no traffic occurred. Only one long, empty train, which evinced no signs of stirring, still extended the length of the platform. I had thought the service was more frequent.

My patience gave way. "I must go through the gates again, and buy something to read!" I soliloquised.

I sauntered down to the book-stall;—

"What periodicals have you?" I asked the boy.

"Eh?" he said.

"What periodicals?" I repeated.

"I don't know what you mean by per——, *periocid-als*, we've got the 'Cape Times!'"

It proved he could hardly have summed up the selection better. During a lengthy survey in search of some familiar wrapper, my gaze encountered nothing but local journalism, and a handful of octogenary novels, English ones of course—I have not come across a novel of Colonial manufacture; after newspapers without news, indeed, and wine without flavour, I am puzzled to discover *anything* they make in the Cape, excepting bread, and they would have *that* imported if they could!

This being my prospect of obtaining amusement at the station, I turned into the streets; possibly I did not know the right places to essay, but at the shops again the "Cape Times" was to all intents and purposes the sole commodity in stock, and with the weekly edition of this exhilarating publication I was finally fain to return to my post of observation, wondering as I retraced my steps if there were any other country upon earth to whom Providence had given so much, and man had done so little.

Meanwhile the sleepy platform had awakened. Passengers and porters hurried to and fro; the aggravatingly motionless train was about to start. Resuming my former situation, and unfolding my purchase that I might see without being perceived, I eagerly scanned the features of the passers-by.

There were men in ordinary round felt hats, and men in canvas helmets, men in slovenly, and men in scrupulous attire. The masculine gender preponderated, and amidst such *embarras de richesse* I was confused.

Suddenly my glance fell on a countenance behind the window of a first-class compartment; it was partially bent as its owner coaxed the flame of a vesta into juxtaposition with his cigar, but I fancied with a leaping of the heart my vigil had borne fruit. The instant that head should be lifted I could feel sure. The green flag waved aloft. It was an anxious moment; would the light reach the cigar, or the guard blow his whistle first?

The signal came, and the tobacco was ignited, for simultaneously with the engine's preparatory snort the head behind the glass was raised, and I saw Jasper Vining steam complacently past me emitting a wreath of smoke.

I could have laughed aloud with joy, the revulsion of feeling from suspense to triumph was so great.

"When is the next train?" was my immediate inquiry. "How long before the next?"

"Are you thinking of waiting for it, ma'am?" rejoined the official I had stopped.

"Well, yes, I was; why do you ask?"

"Only because you'll have a precious long time to wait," he responded coolly, "that's all!"

"I don't understand you; I thought the Wynberg trains left frequently?"

"'Wynberg'!" he said. "*That's* the platform for Wynberg on the other side, not this!"

"Not this?" I echoed. "Then,—then," the whole mistake I had committed dawning across me, "where does that train go, just left? Tell me quickly, I have made some blunder; what train was that?"

"That," he answered as he grinned like an idiot, "was the Diamond Fields express!"

And the cause of my discomfiture was in my hand! There, when I lay prostrate on the couch in the hotel; there, when I was foiled in the very second of success; there, in those audacious, monstrous, prying columns positively forced upon me and printed for every pair of eyes in the town to see, Dunstan espied the following item of intelligence:

"List of Passengers per S.S. 'Drummond Castle:'" amongst them

"Mrs. Lea, (and maid)."

## CHAPTER X

QUEEN'S HOTEL,
*Kimberley,*
*December 12th.*

I AM on the Diamond Fields of South Africa; I had a flying survey of desolate tracts of "veldt" (pronounced

"felt") and straggling settlements where the "population" rushed open-mouthed to gaze upon this mode of
locomotion, which was still a novelty to them. I medi-
tated the will-o'-the-wisp chase I had undertaken was
indeed leading me to strange encampments, and con-
soled myself by reflecting the limit of that man's retreat
must now be reached unless he elected to withdraw further into the interior, and domicile himself in Zululand
among the "Kraals."

I had a glimpse from the railway-carriage of a sun-
set as vivid as ever Turner depicted to an incredulous
world; and then I did what I have never done before at
any place I came to,—I walked straight to the door of
my destination, and looked out.

What did I see! A large open space where teams of
oxen lay wallowing in dust three inches deep; to the
right and left of me a row of one-storied shops and
canteens, their corrugated-iron roofs blazing in the
sun. I saw hot-faced, wearied men threading their way
between the waggons to the post office close by, issu-
ing with brighter eyes, and letters in their clutch; or
empty-handed and hopeless, to slowly drag their feet
across the loathsome sand again. I saw within half a
yard of me that which would necessitate me announcing my presence here as "Mrs. Lea," *nolens volens*, and

made the new-found *alias* under which I had this time travelled unavailing,—Jasper Vining himself!

I do not know which of us was the more startled, he or I; there was no excuse for us avoiding each other, there we were standing near enough to shake hands.

It was better to recognise him, and I bowed. "How do you do?" I said, advancing a step, with a million possibilities of disaster whirling through my brain; "we have met before, though we have never been introduced!"

"And what an original *rencontre!*" he faltered, paling. "My name is 'Vane,—Vane'; yours I overheard in Lisbon from your maid. I have the pleasure of speaking to Mrs. Lea, I believe?"

"Yes; we seem fated to dispense with *les convenances*, do we not? She is there now, my maid, I mean, seeing to the luggage. I had no idea we should ever meet again here!"

I did not know what to talk about, I was frightened of uttering the wrong thing; yet now it had proved impracticable to keep the fact that I had followed him secret, it was essential to make conversation of some sort, and if possible to dispel suspicion.

"May I ask if you have been here long, Mr.—Vane? At least, how foolish, I need not of course; unless you were ubiquitous you hardly could! Isn't it curious we should both have been on the point of sailing for the Cape, and neither supposed it of the other?"

Why would not the man say something; he kept staring at me as if I had dropped from the skies! "Oh," I ejaculated, "here *is* Dunstan! Is everything all right, Dunstan?" I had a vague notion she might cry out when she saw him. "I am told I shall find the Queen's Hotel comfortable, shall I?"

"Have you not come to join your husband then?" he exclaimed, "that is, have you no relations here?"

"None whatever; I am a widow;" I answered sadly: "it is a long tale the business that brought me to Kimberley, I must tell it to you another time if you will allow me!"

I certainly could not have told him at once; it was not invented.

"In that case"—and I admired him for his pluck, he shook off his stupefaction, and confronted me 'game'; "in that case you cannot do better than go to 'The Queen's,' Mrs. Lea. I shall feel honoured by your confidence,—I am staying in that hotel myself!"

So it happened that, of all persons upon earth, it was the absconder I had been seeking who put us courteously into one of those two-horse cabs, and gave instructions for our heavier portmanteaux to be delivered in the course of the afternoon; that it was to no less an individual than himself I played after dinner, and that it was to Vining *alias* Vane I was presently confiding a detailed explanation of my errand (evolved in the interval).

"Then you really undertook so stupendous a journey to——"

"To 'gather materials,' Mr. Vane; that's the expression we writers employ! Does it sound ridiculous?"

"On the contrary, most praiseworthy; I had no idea when I read a description of a place in a novel that I could regard it as real. You quite restore my faith in human nature!"

"Oh, we seldom venture to take our heroes into countries we have not visited ourselves; the reviews might be awkward, you know!"

I thought it would be more awkward when he found out instead of writing stories I only told them, but then an inevitable part of the vocation I had entered was to lie.

"And do you propose remaining long?"

"That will of course depend on circumstances; I hope *not* very long!" I answered with exceeding truth this time. "I am afraid you are encouraging me to make myself a nuisance though. I shall be tempted to ask you what is the most worth seeing, and rely upon you as on a kind of colonial 'Baedecker'!"

"I shall be delighted to place myself at your service, Mrs. Lea; I have any amount of leisure at present, but of course I've been here rather a short while to act the *cicerone* with great effect!"

"If you are sure I shall not be troubling you," I said doubtfully, "you would really be assisting me very much!" and so it was settled.

Later, when Dunstan and I discussed this unlooked-for turn of affairs we decided the chance encounter had after all been fortunate. Whatever distrust he might have he had evidently determined to put a bold front on it, and no matter how much he might be on his guard the intimacy was bound to afford me more opportunities of bringing my mission to a successful issue than the conduct of my investigations from a distance such as I had originally contemplated. On the whole then it was in no despondent frame of mind that I retired to my room at the close of my first day on the Diamond Fields.

The next afternoon he came in to luncheon while I was there; as I had found out the night before our table was the same, and in the course of the meal he offered to procure me a 'pass' to inspect a mine.

"You can go down, if you like, Mrs. Lea," he said, "but I would not advise it, the way wants knowing!"

"Thank you," I replied, "I think I'll content myself with viewing the machinery on the top; I should not care to be whirled down the wires in one of those buckets I saw the men clinging to an hour or two ago!"

Oh, you wouldn't be asked to do that," he laughed; "there *is* a pathway, though it isn't quite so level as the Brighton pier! Still you will see quite enough up above to make your head ache, I can promise you; the 'sorting' is most interesting, that is the process in which they find the stones."

"Can I go with Dunstan?"

"Certainly, I will try to get a pass for three; that may include me in the *rôle* of guide, philosopher, and friend?"

The faint stress he laid upon the last article of the inventory was slightly embarrassing, but I nodded a quick assent.

"I should be ungrateful to say 'no'; if you will come too, and explain, I shall naturally be pleased. Men always understand more of these things than women, and the glimpse I was able to obtain of it from the market showed me a 'key' was a necessary adjunct!"

"Then as 'key' or 'friend' I am to make one of the party; very well, Mrs. Lea, I will hunt up all the diggers I have met, and endeavour to get the desired paper from somebody. This evening you shall hear the result; in the meantime, *au revoir!*"

I wish he had not spoken of being my friend; it makes me feel mean!

*      *      *      *      *

*December 19th.*

During the last six days, ever since that expedition indeed, a thought has come to me which I have sufficient conscience to find distressing. Whatever doubts he may have had earlier, I do not believe the man suspects me now.

Were I wise, this, so far from troubling me, should be a very reassuring idea, for, if a fact, it must greatly simplify my task. I know that, I keep telling myself so, but there is another side to the picture: to take advantage of his good faith is hardly a lady's mode of action.

He is a thief; he himself has betrayed confidence; more, he has broken the law! I want to remember it; I want to retain the knowledge in my memory, and not allow it to slip away from me for so much as a minute, because (it is an ignominious, puerile confession) I am beginning to regard myself as only one degree less vile!

It is terribly silly; here is the fulfilment of those prospects I have painted in my most sanguine moods; I grasp the very chance I have looked forward to, and built upon; and now that all my hopes and prayers are answered I falter within a week, because, forsooth, it is not honourable!

What honour had *he*? What scruples did he permit to come between *him* and his design? Then why should his punishment be retarded by such feelings as he cannot comprehend! He had income, position, and respect; all the things that make life worth living, and ——; no, I am wrong, not all! There is one desideratum more, and sweeter: that something I have gone without since a dull October day, ah, how many years ago, when, an ill-dressed pale-faced girl, they took me aside at school, and said coldly:

"Be very grateful to Heaven and to us, because we are going to keep you here out of charity; you have no longer a mother, she is dead!"

But he may have had love too, as well as he had the rest. I see no cause why I should pity him; I am not going to suggest so false a sentiment! He is to suffer for his crime in prison, and, as for me, my course is mapped out: I am to be the medium to put the hand-cuffs round his wrists. All the reflection in the world cannot alter it.

I must write my Report for the mail!

## CHAPTER XI

*January 9th, 1888.*

"I CAN hardly believe you have been here a month, Mrs. Lea," he said to me this morning; "it seems impossible!"

"I suppose that is a compliment, seeing how much of your time out of that month you have spared to me," I rejoined; "is it meant for one?"

We were in the large apartment overlooking Stockdale Street, and I was standing half on the balcony, half on the rug, thinking how shamefully neglected this record of mine had been.

"And yet," he continued after a pause, "it appears much longer, too, since you and I met!"

"Why, so it is," I answered; "didn't we say 'how do you do' in Lisbon more than as long ago again? Yours isn't half a paradox! By-the-bye, that reminds me, I have never returned your property, often as I've promised it; I have brought it down to give to you now,—permit me, with many thanks!"

"What, the handkerchief,—you are indeed conscientious!"

"Honesty's the best policy——"

"'*In small things*,' as some infidel added!" he remarked, as he took it from my hand. "There's a good deal of philosophy in that postscript, Mrs. Lea!"

"Dangerous philosophy, I opine, when it leads to confusion between *meum* and *tuum!*"

"I daresay," he sighed; "I haven't tested it! How is your book progressing?"

"My book! Oh, the only composition I am engaged on, unless you except correspondence, has scarcely been touched since I arrived. I began it, meaning to write a portion every day, but weeks go by sometimes without my opening it; more good intentions broken, you see!"

"The end of most good intentions! You've not shocked me, I'm to a certain extent a fatalist, a big word which only means I am able to perceive destiny is stronger than human beings! You won't dispute that?"

"I am not going to, at any rate, but don't construe silence into consent; that one is a mistake like the majority of proverbs!"

"Though you just had recourse to them yourself!"

"The privileged inconsistency of my sex!"

"Play something?" he requested abruptly, going across to the piano.

"I don't care to, here," I replied; "you saw how the people stared the first evening; we are not on the continent!"

"But there is no one in now; the few women there are have gone out, and none of the men will be back till *tiffin!*"

"I'd sooner you did not ask me, I don't want to make myself conspicuous!"

"As you please!" he responded, with a shrug of the shoulders.

I took the seat he had placed for me, and without premeditation strayed into the most exquisite of all Chopin's *nocturnes*, the second; that melody wherein the mournful dissatisfaction which is its keynote thrice rises in the treble until the culminating D-flat comes like a veritable sob of pain, and, in playing, I was thinking of this man's wasted life. The advantages he had flung away ceased to double his offence, they made the wreck more pitiable; I thought what he might have been under better influences, and what he was in fact, an exile and a fugitive.

Then by a swift transition only explicable by the dominion self wields over our holiest moods, and by no association of ideas, my fancy sped back to Seville; I was remembering how from my window I had watched a beggar over there, and envied him. He was blind, he was in rags, and yet I envied him, for a little child would lead him to his post in early morning, and put up her baby lips to kiss him when she left. One day the beggar did not come. He was dead. Then the child would come alone, and cry upon the step where he had been used to sit. "Who would cry for *me* if I were dead?" I had murmured. "What voice would falter as it spoke my name?—How silly, not one would even speak it!"

For the last time came that wail mounting in *crescendo*, and I wondered vaguely if I had been given a brother whether all would have been still the same. I yearned for the clasp of this unborn brother's arms to help and protect me; to feel I had someone to say to me "This is right, and that is wrong;" if I had had a brother I might have been a softer woman.

"Thank you," said my companion earnestly, "thank you very much!" My fingers rested on the final chord.

For a moment I had a wild impulse to tell him what I was, and bid him hate me; only the recollection of the trust I should be violating held me back.

"It is beautiful, that *nocturne*, is it not?"

"Yes," he assented, "like much of Chopin's music, it says for us all we feel but do not know how to say ourselves!"

"It moved you like that too?" I exclaimed.

"I felt whilst you were at the piano, Mrs. Lea, that I was unutterably base, and that I might be superlatively good; contradictory emotions, but simultaneous and sincere!"

"And also evanescent! It is the same with all of us; we see "Jo" at the theatre, and give half-a-crown to the first vagabond we notice outside the doors, but the next day we are ourselves again, and pass the mother with six children selling groundsel without remorse. Art is very potent, but human nature is much more mean!"

"Yet surely there are circumstances under which one may become better, don't you think so?"

"I am twenty-eight years old, Mr. Vane, but unhappily I haven't found them!"

"You wrong yourself sometimes," he said; "you do indeed, nature never intended you for a cynic!"

"Unfortunately," I answered, rising, "it is not nature's intention which moulds us, but the world's lesson. There, pray don't let us go in for drawing-room metaphysics, they generally mean egotism with a long name!"

"I want to be egotistical," he proceeded calmly; "don't go yet, I want to talk to you about myself, may I? I do not know why I should inflict my private affairs on you, I'm not often taken communicative, upon my word, but I suppose the desire for sympathy comes to most men sometimes, and it certainly comes to me when I'm with you!"

"I am much too selfish a person to make an ideal *confidante*," I rejoined awkwardly; "I warn you before-hand!"

"But I won't be warned; and if you were half as bitter as you pretend, you would attract me so, I could never admire a feminine edition of myself! I want advice, I've made an awful mess of my life, that's a fact; to put it in its mildest form, I've been a fool. There are some things one can't speak of without glossing over to a woman, more especially a woman whose opinion one values; but a short while back

I, in an unexpected fashion, came into a lot of money——"

"A legacy?" I faltered.

"Eh? Oh, yes, a legacy; well, I ran through the whole heap in a few months, played general ducks and drakes with it till I found myself almost broke, and then, in the manner of the bad little boy who went fishing on Sunday, and seasonably repented when he fell in the pool, I determined to cut the whole game, the cards, and the turf, and the tables, turn over a new leaf, and begin afresh. Now do you believe a man who has come a cropper can blot the page out, and make amends for—for a terrible folly?"

What was I to say! His gaze pained me, and the sunshine hurt my eyes; what *could* I say that would not be a mockery?

"Do you think it is too late?"

"They say it is never too late for good resolutions," I replied harshly; "I hope for all our sakes the axiom may be true!"

"I have at least a chance of doing something," he resumed; "one of the mining companies is to be let; rich ground, by all accounts, and only vacant through a heavy fall of reef which the present lessees can't afford to haul out. There's a possibility of my going into it in partnership with a fellow who has all the business at his fingers' ends; if our tender should be accepted, Mrs. Lea, I may be a rich man again!"

"You have made an offer for the lease?"

"Yes," he responded cheerfully. "I ought to have enough for my share of the starting capital, and if I should require more, I hope to be able to raise it!"

The gong sounded as he imparted this piece of information, and we went down. All the progress I have made in the past three weeks is comprised in the interview just chronicled. I lay my head on the pillow with the knowledge of having gained the confidence of the man I am going to ruin, and of course I am glad and proud. Dunstan wearies me with questions and prognostications of success, her cruel satisfaction makes it a relief to be alone.

I have not seen him since two o'clock. I wish that I might never see him any more!

&ast;  &ast;  &ast;  &ast;  &ast;

*January 16th.*

His tender was the highest, and he is already hard at work; we never meet in the daytime now, excepting for a few minutes at *tiffin*, when he comes in hot and dusty, and looking, oh, so dreadfully tired. The weather is growing insupportable, it was 110° in the shade to-day.

They say there is a terrible illness, to which Europeans are particularly liable during their first summer here, known as 'Camp fever,' and that it is often contracted by too reckless exposure to the sun. During the last four days I have missed a woman, who used to sit at the table opposite to mine; this morning I inquired the reason of her absence, they said "Camp fever!" This evening I asked if she was better; they answered she was dead.

What if *he* should fall ill in this fearful place without a friend to nurse him! What if, like that poor woman,—

Oh, why did I not starve with my self-respect before I became a spy! What is it to me he is a scoundrel, does his criminality lessen my degradation? Who was the author of the precept, There can be no friendship without respect? False every word of it! For if it is not friendship I have for this man what is it? why am I trembling at that horrid thought which crossed my mind? Why do I feel I would gladly take his guilt upon my shoulders, work for him, suffer for him, so that he, my friend, should be innocent and free?

Beautiful sentiment, proverbial and profound philosophy culled from our first French grammar, I bow before your wisdom:

*"L'amitié est une belle fleur dont l'estime est la tige!"*

## CHAPTER XII

*January 23rd.*

I HAVE had a frightful dream, a dream that makes my bed an object of terror; I could not go to sleep again if I tried.

Under these circumstances I have lighted the lamp, and prepared myself to wait for morning; it is not quite four a.m., and I want to write this dream of mine down, just as all the incidents occurred while they are still frightening me in recollection by their semblance of reality.

I was in a wide, strange road; I knew it was the Du-Toits-Pan-road, for I had been in it often, and yet it was unfamiliar. The light was dim, I think it must have been dawn, since it was the same light as is breaking over the house-tops now. There were two men with me, and I was leading them. They said, "Is this the way?" and I answered "Yes, this is the way; you must follow me!" My feet sank deep in dust; it hampered my movements, and made each step an effort. It seemed to me I must be very ill. I could see nothing but dust in front of me, excepting a low fringe of stunted bushes far away. The men murmured "We shall be late!" I shook my head. I said, "We are there!"

We had come to a great building, and we entered it; we passed silently through long passages lined with doors until we came to one different from the rest, a narrow door shaped like a coffin-lid, and studded with nails; this we pushed open, and walked inside.

Within the room the sunshine was streaming hotly through a window, and two arms protruding from a heap upon the floor extended right across the threshold. We knew this heap was a human body lying beneath the coverlet as it had rolled from the bed in pain. The air was black with flies, and they were crawling over the dead hands.

My companions turned to me: "Where have you brought us?" they asked. I cried, "My mission has finished in a hospital ward!"

Then I was kneeling on the ground, I drew the blanket from the face; it was the face of the man I had hunted. Sight came back to the eyeballs that stared up at me; the white lips moved. They whispered, "My sin has parted us! Miriam, my love, have mercy!" I said, "I am going to die with you because I cannot save you. Hold me tight!"

The features of the two men I had guided appeared blurred by distance; I saw myself weeping beside his corpse below, and yet it was not I, for I was floating towards another life bearing him with me, as I had known him in the flesh, breathing and speaking to me. As we ascended nearer to the heavens unclosing to receive us, a vast impenetrable mist sailed between me and the world, sinking earthward as we rose. Still I strained him to me, and we clung together. Denser grew that cloud, and I marvelled what it might be; voices answered, "It is the sins of which one soul is purged!" At the same instant my clasp relaxed, my arms dropped asunder, and the man I loved fell downward beyond my reach, beyond my sight, down—down—down through Space, only his scream re-echoed through the Universe, and I awoke!     ·

\*          \*          \*          \*          \*

*January 25th.*

It was two o'clock, the mining whistles had sounded the hour for recommencing work, and I was sitting alone in the hotel thinking. The impression of that dream was yet upon me; it had haunted me for forty-eight hours with miserable persistency.

I knew now, as absolutely as I had known in the vision, that I loved! that the man I was deceiving had become to me far dearer than my own existence. I knew it was no mere liking or regard for him which made me shudder in the presence of my accomplice, and shrink ashamed under her gaze, but the unadmitted consciousness of a passion that disgraced me. I could not dupe myself; I did not try. If it was shame to care for him it was also sweet! I longed again for the fancied touch of his embrace about my neck, to hear him saying as I had heard him in imagination, "Miriam, my love!" and yet I remembered I must never listen!

"Playing truant, you see, Mrs. Lea!" The door had opened, and the object of my thoughts crossed the room to where I sat.

"Why, yes," I exclaimed, starting, "I heard the whistles some time ago."

"I daresay," he answered; "the fact is there is nothing to be done this afternoon, so I mean to stop up here, and spoil your reverie."

"How do you know I am going to stay at home?"

"Oh, come," he remonstrated, "you won't pretend you had any idea of taking a stroll, with the thermometer making rapid progress towards boiling-point? I've been looking forward to this 'half-holiday' all the morning, Mrs. Lea,—don't be unkind! Why have you chosen that corner right in the sun; let me make it more comfortable for you!"

He pulled down the blind, and drew the curtains across the window, screening me from the glare.

"Next a cushion," he observed; "there, is that better, and will you stay now?"

"Thank you," I replied, "you are very good!"

"The mail is in, and I have brought you some of the English journals," he continued. "I always think they are welcome out here myself; there are conditions under which a comic-paper may become the connecting link of hemispheres,—see!"

"And after working harder than the niggers since sunrise you actually took the trouble to walk about the camp buying those for me?"

"No, I did not, because it wasn't a trouble! It occurred to me as I was loafing in the engine-house throwing pebbles at the boiler (arduous occupation, was it not?). I said, 'By Jove, the mail's due; if it's delivered before I go back to *tiffin* I'll stroll round to the main street, and take that poor little traveller all alone in this *Gott-verlassen* hole something to read.' Behold the result!"

He deposited a bundle of periodicals in my lap, and stood looking down at me as I turned them over.

"What is it?" he asked curtly; "you are worrying, tell me why?"

"'Worrying'!" I repeated. "What makes you say that?"

"I am sure of it; you haven't understood a single one of those printed lines, you haven't even attempted to follow them. Tell me what's the matter?"

"There isn't anything the matter; I have a headache, perhaps, that is all,—what should there be?"

"There should be nothing if I could help it!" he said, with his deep grey eyes still fixed on me. "I can't bear to see you wretched, and lately you have been getting quieter every day; when you do laugh, the laugh ends in a sigh. Is it only that the place depresses you, or——"

"Nonsense, are you adding geloscopy to your accomplishments! I'm bored, moping, out of sorts, that's the alarming complaint; Kimberley isn't the most lively town for a stranger,—I wish with my whole soul I'd never come to it!"

He gave that quick gesture of the shoulder which was a habit with him, and might mean anything, and for a while we were both silent. Presently he spoke again.

"That was not a considerate remark you made just now!"

"What wasn't?" I inquired briefly; "I've quite forgotten what I said!"

"Thank you; to refresh your memory, you expressed a profound regret that you had ever come here!"

"Oh, yes, so I did; well, after the preface, the plot:— which was the remark you found inconsiderate?"

"It was that one! Do you suppose it could have been pleasant to hear? Oh, I know you are going to reply that you did not regard me as responsible for Kimberley's defects, that I didn't build it, or with some retort equally ridiculous; but I think you might have kept that very heartfelt sorrow to yourself!"

"It *was* a *gaucherie*," I rejoined coldly, "but there is no occasion to be rude!"

He muttered something complimentary or otherwise under his breath, (probably 'otherwise') and picked out an air with one finger on the piano. I wanted badly to own that if I had meant it it was for his sake; to tell him how he himself must repent our meeting if I dared but hint its cause, but I could not! I had to be dumb, and look indifferent.

The notion crossed my mind that if he should,—should grow to like me before my errand had been completed, how much more vile he would hold me when the blow fell; the thought was wonderful, it was so full of mixed emotions. To be hated by him would be torture, but—to be *loved* by him first! It seemed to me there would be joy enough in that to live upon in recollection through my future of suffering; besides I could always die!

And still that tune went on, jingling upon the sunshine.

But for him, I was only thinking of myself! Would not his punishment be greater if he were fond of the woman who had denounced him? If during those years of miserable atonement he should be deeming every sign of my affection false; be cursing that very utterance in one happy moment, when perhaps I had forgotten, as a trap to lead him to his ruin; greater? Yes, immeasurably more hard!

"Don't let you and me quarrel," he petitioned, closing the instrument with a bang. "I beg your pardon; I didn't know I was so sensitive! By-the-bye, you've not wondered about my being 'off duty,' and after all my industry I expected it was going to create a sensation!"

"Why, is there another reason besides the one you volunteered?"

"Well yes, I didn't go into details; it is true there is nothing much to be done this afternoon, but it's because we have been hauling day and night, got the last load of reef out, and are ready to commence real work as soon as we have more funds. That's good news, I take it?"

"It is, indeed;" I responded, "the claims being cleared you can begin to dig for diamonds, of course?"

"Certainly; we shall soon know the value of the ground now, and if it should yield well—! Will you shake hands, and wish me luck, Mrs. Lea?"

"What do you mean 'As soon as you have more funds?'" I queried, evading the request; "was not the sum you had sufficient?"

"The hauling operations cost more than I had reckoned, but that's of no consequence, I anticipate being able to raise as much as is essential; shake hands and prophesy me fortune, won't you? Tell me I am going to make up for the past, and that it will be my own fault if I'm ever reminded of it!"

"How can I, I——, I'm not a Sibyl," I objected nervously; "how could my prophecy affect you?"

"Never mind," he insisted, "gamblers are notoriously superstitious; view it as a whim of mine if you choose, or think more truly that I want seriously to feel I have your interest as a talisman; think your encouragement would help me on, and your faith in me would be something to justify! Come, Mrs. Lea, it isn't an enormous demand, you will give me your hand, and say what I asked?"

As he stood waiting to clasp it in his own, Dunstan interrupted us, bringing me a letter. The glance I threw at the superscription was unnecessary; it was a letter from my employers.

## CHAPTER XIII

*January 26th.*

MR. BAZALGETTE wrote in reply to the Report from Cape Town by which I had announced my immediate departure for the Fields; and as the amount with which he had furnished me on the eve of my voyage to South Africa had at that date been already so low as to warrant my application for further supplies, he remitted a draft for a hundred and fifty pounds.

A package of dilapidated notes, torn and pinned together, is lying before me on the dressing-table, and I have been sitting here all the morning stonily staring at it with a prayer for strength in my heart; for in cashing that remittance, I have this day seen the detective's prognostications fulfilled, and the object of his instructions offering bonds for sale in the Standard Bank.

I hardly comprehended the meaning of the teller's inquiry, "How will you take it?" I scarcely knew what directions I stammered in response; I only heard that fragment of the low quick colloquy on my right, reaching my ears across the persons who divided us: "When will he be disengaged? I wish to dispose of the bonds without delay, I am pressed for ready-money!"

"One fifty, five tens, and ten fives; you will find that correct, madam!"

Without counting I thrust them into a roll, and hurried out to meditate my mode of action; and yet I have done nothing. I have simply sat and asked for the courage to perform my duty.

The course I should pursue is a very easy one; it is to mail the intelligence to London. Easy—to say; easy and unavoidable according to the dictates of the commonest honour; but there is an influence at work in me stronger than honour, stronger than justice, which bids me pause and draw back while there is still time.

Oh, Heaven help me, what shall I do? Am I to betray the employers whose bread I eat; or am I to consign the man I love to gaol?

Those people in England have paid me, put their trust in me, perhaps saved me from starvation; if I deceived them should I not be the vilest wretch on earth? Gratitude, honesty, everything points one way, all the sophistry in the world cannot blind me to it; the information shall be sent!

The Report is ready for the post; it lies beside me now!

\*     \*     \*     \*     \*

I had barely sealed the envelope when I heard a step in the next room,—it was *his*. As I joined him he came towards me evidently agitated by some joyful event; I had not to wait long to know the cause.

"Look," he exclaimed triumphantly, "our first 'find'!"

It was a two-hundred-and-fifty-carat stone discovered in the mine an hour before. Massive and pure, without a flaw or spot, it might be expected to realize, he told me, perhaps five thousand pounds; no wonder he was pleased.

"You see," he laughed, "you are bringing me luck whether you will or no!"

Bringing him luck, I!

"If it should sell so well as that, it will be two-thou-sand-five-hundred to my share; no fortune, as I reck-oned once, worth having now, though!" he continued; "Mrs. Lea, a diamond company is the finest gamble I've ever tried!"

He was like a child with a new toy; he kept spinning it on the cloth, and holding it up to gaze at it against the light. "Wait till it's cut," he repeated again and again, "it'll be magnificent!" Then suddenly he threw it back upon the table, and said quite seriously:

"Are you glad?"

"I should be glad if you could remain as happy as you are at this minute," I replied, and it was true.

"Do you mean that?" he questioned. "It rests with you to make me always much happier!"—"No, now you must listen to me; I didn't intend to say it yet, I had made up my mind to wait until I had something to offer, but I *can't* wait, and you shan't *go!* I love you,—pshaw, what does that tell you? The first syllables we learn to speak are 'I love,' and we go on wearing them threadbare for the rest of our lives; what I want you to understand is that you are more to me than any woman I ever met, that you fill every one of my thoughts and hopes. You *are* my hopes; do you suppose I cared for this trumpery stone for its own sake? I cared for it for yours, because when that hulking nigger brought it over to me in the claims it seemed to be one step the nearer you! Oh, I have no right to ask it; to win you is the maddest thing a man in my position ever dreamed, but you'd be sorry for me if you guessed how I have cursed myself lately for that folly you know about; how I have wished we could have come together before it happened. Tell me you forgive me not being strong enough to stand by and run the risk of losing you; tell me you will forget how broke I am, and be my wife?"

"I cannot, it is impossible," I answered thickly, "I entreat you not to say any more!"

My temples were throbbing; I loathed myself and my existence, everything but him I was sending from me, and yet how could I make the dismissal less harsh?

"Is my mistake irreparable?" he pleaded still; "won't you believe I would work for you, and get something back? I would, I swear it; you should never be deprived of the comforts you are used to, I would never deny you a single request!"

"It isn't that, ah don't talk of money! What do you imagine me to be, a successful writer? I am a beggar; not one line of mine will ever be in print. I am a nobody without income, and without prospects, but nothing can alter my decision; it is useless for you to persist!"

"Do you care for anybody else?"

"What does it matter for whom I care; you will leave me, and only remember me to wonder how you could have been so weak!"

"Do you care for anybody else? Truthfully, with your eyes to mine, is there someone you like better?"

"I have no one to be fond of in the world," I faltered, "no one to be fond of me; now go!"

"No, I will not go," he said fiercely; "you have confessed the reason you refuse! You fancy because we are both poor you would be a drag on me, and I should one day be brute enough to regret your sacrifice; you are wrong! Mrs. Lea—, to think I should not even know your name! What is it? graceful, and yet hard too, the same as you can be,—tell me!"

"It is 'Miriam.'"

"A beautiful one," he murmured gravely; "it sounds like a prayer! Miriam, my life is for you to guide; give yourself to me, and I will be worthy of your trust; reject me, and I shall be a failure to the end! Don't let false pride rob me of you, my dear; don't reply 'no' without trying to say 'yes.' A woman is very powerful when she is as much to a man as you to me, and you are able now, because I love you, to shape my whole future with a word!"

"You are cruel to urge that," I retorted; "it is unfair!"

"Perhaps," he rejoined, "but it is easy to be brave when you are mistress of the situation; the very consciousness which strengthens you makes me a coward! It must be always so, the man can only crave; a caprice may turn him away hopeless; a sentence is to decide his fate; can you blame him for appealing to all that is best in the nature of the girl who is to speak it! Sweetheart, am I to go from here miserable or blessed? Determine; be yourself, throw off the wretched cynicism that hides your real mind, and let us fight our difficulties together, boldly, side by side!"

He was supplicating for more than he divined; he was begging his escape of me, me who could save him! The knowledge made that petition an agony to hear; I could merely signify my resolution by a gesture.

"I can't describe my feelings," he cried, "I'm not sufficiently clever; I never found out how impotent speech was until I wanted it to express my soul. Grant me the opportunity, and I will prove my earnestness by my deeds! Each act shall be a witness of my sincerity, and an effort to deserve you. Darling, won't you have faith?"

The capability for pain was passing from me at last; I was beginning to listen almost apathetically, as under an anæsthetic one may bear some horrible operation. Now I waited dumbly for the trial to finish.

"Well," he resumed coldly, "I will not sue any more; you are inflexible, and I have humbled myself enough! Good-bye,—do we part friends?"

Was it to be interminable? I could have flung myself at this man's feet, but I might not aver I was his friend! I could only implore his pardon mutely, and wait to be alone. Heaven can testify the glance was not intended for encouragement, yet it must have revealed my suffering.

The sternness died from his gaze, and he strode towards me; he seized me by the wrists, and drew me to him:

"Miriam, my love, have mercy!"

The phrase broke from him that had been borne upon me in my dream. The room with its brackets and its mirrors seemed swimming round me as I strove to wrench myself free, and still he grasped me firmly, beseeching, and upbraiding me by turns. "Do you hate me?" he queried passionately, "is the doctrine of affinity such a lie that I whom you can influence for good or bad, sway like a child according to your will, am only able to inspire an antipathy in you? There is no sacrifice you could demand I would not deem it a privilege to make if it brought me your thanks; there isn't a task I would shrink from if you said to me 'do it, I shall be pleased;' and yet I am so utterly nothing to you I cannot move you a hair's breadth, that my distress doesn't even excite your pity! Is it that I love you so absolutely you despise me, or is it indeed that you have no sensibility to be touched? I can compel you to be passive, that is all; I can clasp your hands, and detain you by sheer physical force as I do now, but you, the real you who attracted me, are as far away from me as ever, and I hold a piece of stone!"

I did not attempt to release myself any longer; the limits of endurance had been reached. I was guilty, I was wicked, but I was a woman, and I loved him! I lifted my face to his, and the joy I saw in it out-balanced the cognizance of sin. He caught me in his arms till my head lay upon his shoulder, and our lips met.

"You consent to marry me?"

"Yes," I said, "you have conquered; I am willing to be your wife!"

And now that he has left me, I am revolving that promise, and the shame to which it pledges me. I have no excuse to offer, I am committing an infamous action, and I am aware of it; I may even be amenable to the law; let them punish me,—they shall never have him! I have done with scruples and conscience, and I will shield him against them all; no information of mine——! God! I had forgotten the Report! * * *

Dunstan has posted it, the letter has gone!

## CHAPTER XIV

*February 14th.*

I HAVE had time to meditate on that catastrophe while watching beside a sick-bed; Dunstan has been very ill. A fortnight ago her life was despaired of, and we thought Providence had destined another victim of the fever to be buried in this wilderness of sand. Then, when hope was least, the delirium passed; by degrees the awful yellow shade which had overspread her cheeks merged into the pallor of convalescence, and I saw the woman I had known so strong and self-reliant lying back upon the pillows spared, but as helpless as a little babe. She is now well enough to travel, and the doctor recommends the invariable prescription in such cases, a sojourn in the Colony. She will go to Cape Town to-morrow, ignorant of the fact that she and I will never meet again. In a week I shall have betrayed my trust, and saved him who is dearer than my honour. He pressed me to accede to a brief engagement, and I readily consented, for my reflection had shown me it was the wisest plan; that intelligence is only now due in England; the reply cannot be delivered till three weeks hence; by then we shall have quitted Kimberley, and escaped together!

This illness of the companion I am deceiving served as a pretext; I told him I was frightened to remain. At my request he agreed to abandon his work here, and to forsake the place. He will soon be secure in another country, without even surmising the danger he has run.

I mean to restore to Mr. Bazalgette the accumulation of the salary I have drawn, with an enclosure simply bearing my name; I have considered everything, I do not think there is anything else!

*        *        *        *        *

*February 16th.*

Five mornings more to drag themselves away; I count the hours! Dunstan's departure has removed the only obstacle to my design; when I shook hands with her at the station I felt ashamed. The dust is hissing along the streets, and darkening the windows; my very diary is gritty. I have been glancing through its pages, back to the first line of all; what a change since the evening in London when I scribbled it!

I can see the narrow room where I sat, as plainly as if I were in it now; I can remember myself nibbling the pen, and staring out at the opposite houses, wondering if I should ever find anything to do. It is funny that renewing the acquaintance of one's old self, and yet it is melancholy.

Ours will be a curious marriage, as it has been a strange betrothal; we shall leave the hotel together and unaccompanied. What do we want of friends when each of us can bring sufficience to the other? On the 21st, the anniversary of my birth, I commence a new existence dedicated to my husband; our hearts will hide their bitterness, but everything save two secrets that are pain we give and share. I do not dread the prospect: dread! Were my deserts as infinite as the bounty of Heaven it could vouchsafe no greater blessing than this which crowns a crime!

I wish I had not said that; it sounds like a boast! It makes me tremble lest on the verge of fulfilment I should be reminded of it. What has Heaven to do with me,—with us? To beg its aid, would be a blasphemy;—I cannot see to write, I am crying.—Oh, how helpless is a woman deprived of the resource of prayer!

\*  \*  \*  \*  \*

*February 20th.*
*(Midnight.)*

He left me an hour ago, and I am alone. It is my wedding-eve; the bare hooks, the strapped trunk, the gaping dressing-bag, everything in the apartment appears to announce it. There is nobody to congratulate me, not a voice to say a kind word, yet in twelve hours I shall be a wife.

It is curious I should feel the loneliness of my position more acutely this evening, when it is nearly over, than I have done at any other period of my life; but I seem to be bestowing so worthless a gift in going to him as a woman whom no one will miss.

I suppose most girls on such a night whisper their thoughts into a mother's ear: I have no mother, or I should like to forget my girlhood is past, and to kneel to her now as I used when I was a child!—I had better shut the window, and undress,—how quiet it is!—The breeze blows as softly as your kisses, dear,—I stretch my hands towards you through the mist!—If the spirits of the dead can listen, if they can intercede for the beings they cherished upon Earth, mother, oh, my dead mother up there amongst the stars, ask the Creator you behold to protect the man I love!

\*       \*       \*       \*       \*

*February 21st.*

I am ready,—absurdly early, but I was restless. Three attempts to read the "Independent" have resulted in failure. I am too unsettled to concentrate my attention on a newspaper, and my diary is the sole occupation available.

There has been a letter from Dunstan; she writes she is already a great deal stronger, and trusts to be back in time 'to witness Mr. Vining's arrest.' I tore the epistle into fifty pieces,—why did it not get lost in the post! I have forwarded his money to Mr. Bazalgette, retaining only twenty-five pounds; I cannot decide why I kept that; I do not fancy I am avaricious, however bad I may be otherwise, nevertheless some motive I could not analyse impelled me to pause before I determined to make myself quite a pauper.

The chambermaid has wished me happiness, I am so glad; somebody has said something pleasant at last. I had rung for a cup of tea, and in removing the tray she loitered to such an extent that I glanced round; she turned very red, and murmured:

"I hope it isn't a liberty, ma'am, but what I've got to say is, may you be happy, ma'am, you and the gentleman too!"

I could have hugged that girl, smudges and all! And we *shall* be happy, he and I; remorse has ceased to oppress me, I have flung it from me with the fragments of that hateful letter; I am merely terrified at the magnitude of my joy. I could scarcely pin my

bonnet on, my fingers shook so; and to persuade myself
it is later than the clock will allow I have buttoned my
gloves. My costume is not much like a bride's. I wonder if he will think I look nice!—I hope he will think
I look nice,—the veil does not come far down if he
wants to!

How incomprehensible it is a man should have the
power of altering the whole current of my ideas as he
has done; I am as pliable under his influence as if I were
sixteen! The hardest attendant upon matureness, it
strikes me, is to love deeply, and be conscious the while
that the display of your subjection must always have
the appearance of aping juvenility.

It is a problem, also, what attributes, impercep-
tible to herself, a woman possesses to exert so subtle
a dominion over the man. What does *he* see in *me?*
perhaps——

There is a knock at the door, can it be—? No, it
is the servant again; she has brought me a telegram.
A telegram! Who can have—. Oh, why did I not take
this contingency into account? What a *fool* I was not
to remember they might wire! It must be a *cablegram*
from London, the answer I had calculated to avoid. My
tones are tremulous as I thank her: does she notice my
agitation? She stares, I fancy, and leaves it on the table.

I have not the nerve to open it; it chills me as though it had come to part us even now; Mr. Bazalgette himself seems near; that orange-coloured missive denotes danger,—I will throw it away!

What cowardice, am I mad! My weakness may be imperilling *him*; suppose duplicate instructions have been cabled to the Kimberley police. I must break the seal, and quickly. My darling, I need all my courage now, for you;—the enclosure lies before me!

I struggle to understand it, and I cannot, the cipher has escaped my memory. I am going cold as ice,—wait! The signs grow clear, the sense steals over me. Word for word I translate it; word for word the message handed to me on my wedding morning means:

"Jasper Vining was arrested by Scotland Yard people yesterday in New York. Return. You have been following the wrong man!"

## CHAPTER XV

FOR minutes I sit gazing at it numbed. I keep repeating the sentence mechanically aloud; I hardly master its significance.

"I have been following the wrong man?" That is to say I have been misled by a chance resemblance to a

photograph? I do not know Jasper Vining at all? I have
never seen him?—I cannot grasp it! "He was arrested
in New York yesterday?" Then I have met a man whose
name is what he states it to be; whose only fault is the
venial folly he candidly admitted, the squandering of
an inheritance which might have been a competency.
Is it a dream?

But the bonds?—Again how absolutely I have been
blinded by my own convictions! why did I leap at the
conclusion they must be the stolen bonds when I did not
even hear they were Egyptian? He is sinless; stupefaction fades, and the full import of the revelation crowds
upon me at length. Danger does not threaten either
him or me. Heaven be praised, his innocence removes
every cause for fear, the path is open before us. Stop!
First I must proclaim the truth. My concealment of
the circumstances which brought us together has been
practised, from the time I abjured my mission and its
claims, as much for his sake as my own; whatever my
offence towards my employers, I have since then at least
been staunch to him; but that is over now. He is not
Jasper Vining; he is a gentleman; and reticence after
this would not be delicacy any more, it would be guilt.

My exultance is transient; it ebbs from me, and is
succeeded by a sensation of blank dismay. I have been

"staunch,"—to whom? To Mr. Jack Vane: what will that avail me? I feel suddenly as if I were betrothed to a stranger; I shall be more degraded in his sight by that very treachery than if I had been just. I have only been his equal while I imagined him a thief, and he will refuse to marry me.

Acknowledgment will deal the death-blow to my own future; confession is equivalent to telling the man I love I am no longer fit to be his wife; I will not do this thing, I cannot, no woman could!

Why should I not keep silence still? It would be a safe course; Dunstan must be apprized of the intelligence, and she will return to England; exposure could never overtake me, and I can be his wife in spite of all,—Jack's wife! Ah, have I no honour left? Have I sunk low enough to be disloyal to *him? No!* Ten thousand "noes."—Not that! I will make the avowal, and I will go away; only I cannot speak it! I am going to be honest; I am going to do what is right;—but it must be a letter! I am no heroine, I am flesh and blood, and with all the capabilities of flesh and blood I am suffering now; to make the declaration with my own lips, and to watch the disgust upon his face would kill me.

It is fortunate I reserved some money, it will take me from him. What is the time? There is no room for delay; the note must be written at once. Let me collect my thoughts!—Hark, there are steps in the passage,—they are stopping; I am too late, the ordeal I wanted to shun is at hand. I close my diary; he is outside; I shall not look at it again. It might have finished better, but I shall never pen another entry while I live. He is calling to me,—oh, my heart—

Come in!

    \*      \*      \*      \*      \*

    \*      \*      \*      \*      \*

God is very good: Jack kissed me!

THE END.

Other fiction titles available from British Library Publishing

# THE NOTTING HILL MYSTERY

Charles Warren Adams

'The book is both utterly of its time and utterly ahead of it.'
Paul Collins, *New York Times Book Review*

*The Notting Hill Mystery* is widely considered to be the first ever detective novel. Published in 1864, the dramatic story is told by insurance investigator Ralph Henderson, who is building a case against the sinister Baron 'R___', suspected of murdering his wife. Presented in the form of diary entries, family letters, chemical analysis reports and interviews with witnesses, the novel displays innovative techniques that would not become common features of detective fiction until the 1920s. This new edition of *The Notting Hill Mystery* will be welcomed by all fans of detective fiction.

ISBN 978 0 7123 5859 0
312 pages, 8 black-and-white illustrations

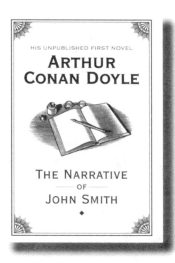

# THE NARRATIVE OF JOHN SMITH

Arthur Conan Doyle

'this early piece crackles with the burning curiosity that Doyle brought to all his activities ... sheds fascinating light on the mind of its creator' David Grylls, *Sunday Times*

In 1883, when he was just 23, Arthur Conan Doyle wrote his first novel *The Narrative of John Smith* while he was living in Portsmouth and struggling to establish himself as both a doctor and a writer. The manuscript remained among his papers and this is its first publication. Many of the themes and stylistic tropes of his later writing, including his first Sherlock Holmes story, *A Study in Scarlet* (1887), can clearly be seen in this book. Though unfinished, *The Narrative of John Smith* stands as a fascinating record of the early work of a man on his way to becoming one of the best-known authors in the world.

ISBN 978 0 7123 5841 5
144 pages, Also available as an ebook (978 0 7123 6301 3)

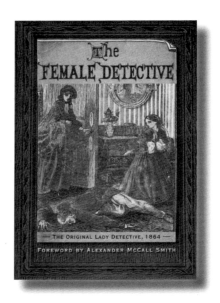

# THE FEMALE DETECTIVE

Andrew Forrester

With a Foreword by Alexander McCall Smith

'Miss Gladden' is the first ever professional female detective to feature in a crime novel. She is a determined and resourceful figure who pursues mysterious cases with ingenuity and skills of logic and deduction. *The Female Detective* was first published in 1864, and it was one of only two novels featuring a female detective to be published at this time – further stories featuring women detectives would not be widely published until later in the century. The reappearance of the original female detective will be welcomed by all fans of detective fiction.

ISBN 978 0 7123 5878 1
328 pages
Also available as an ebook (978 0 7123 6304 4)

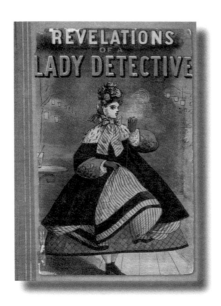

# REVELATIONS OF A LADY DETECTIVE
William Stephens Hayward

With an Introduction by Mike Ashley

Mrs Paschal, the heroine of *Revelations of a Lady Detective,* is only the second ever professional female detective to feature in a work of fiction, pipped to the post by just six months by Andrew Forrester's *The Female Detective.* Mrs Paschal is regularly consulted by the police and serves as an undercover agent as well as investigating her own cases. But even though she is 'verging on forty', she has no hesitation in infiltrating a deadly secret society or casting off her crinolines in order to plummet into a sewer on the trail of a criminal.

ISBN 978 0 7123 5896 5
288 pages
Also available as an ebook (978 0 7123 6305 1)

# THE SANTA KLAUS MURDER

Mavis Doriel Hay

Aunt Mildred declared that no good could come of the Melbury family's Christmas gatherings at their country residence Flaxmere. So when Sir Osmond Melbury, the family patriarch, is discovered – by a guest dressed as Santa Klaus – with a bullet in his head on Christmas Day, the festivities are plunged into chaos. Nearly every member of the party stands to reap some sort of benefit from Sir Osmond's death, but Santa Klaus, the one person who seems to have had every opportunity to fire the shot, has no apparent motive. In the midst of mistrust, suspicion and hatred, it emerges that there was not one Santa Klaus, but two. *The Santa Klaus Murder* is a classic country-house mystery that is now being made available to readers for the first time since its original publication in 1936.

ISBN 978 0 7123 5712 8
288 pages
Also available as an ebook (978 0 7123 6313 6)